PUSHKIN PRESS

SPRING GARDEN

'This gentle story about people brought together by places is like a good meditation: quiet, surprising and deeply satisfying'

New York Times Book Review

'[A] sublime novella of dislocation and regret'

Japan Times

TOMOKA SHIBASAKI was born in 1973 in Osaka and began writing fiction while still in high school. After graduating from university, she took an office job but continued writing, and was shortlisted for the Bungei Prize in 1998. Her first book, *A Day on the Planet*, was turned into a hit movie, and *Spring Garden* won the prestigious Akutagawa Prize in 2014.

POLLY BARTON is a writer and translator of Japanese literature based in Bristol. She was awarded the Fitzcarraldo Essay Prize for her non-fiction debut *Fifty Sounds*, and her second book, *Porn: An Oral History*, was published in 2023. Her recent translations include *Mild Vertigo* by Mieko Kanai, *There's No Such Thing as an Easy Job* by Kikuko Tsumura and *Where the Wild Ladies Are* by Aoko Matsuda.

TOMOKA SHIBASAKI

SPRING GARDEN

translated from the Japanese by
POLLY BARTON

PUSHKIN PRESS

SERIES EDITORS: David Karashima and Michael Emmerich
TRANSLATION EDITOR: Elmer Luke

Pushkin Press
Somerset House, Strand
London WC2R 1LA

HARU NO NIWA by SHIBASAKI Tomoka
Copyright © 2014 by SHIBASAKI Tomoka
All rights reserved.

Original Japanese edition published by Bungeishunju Ltd., Japan

English translation rights in the UK reserved by Pushkin Press,
under the licence granted by SHIBASAKI Tomoka, Japan, arranged
with Bungeishunju Ltd., Japan through Japan UNI Agency, Japan.

English language translation © Polly Barton 2017

First published by Pushkin Press in 2017
This edition first published in 2024

The publisher gratefully acknowledges the support of the British
Centre for Literary Translation and the Nippon Foundation

1 3 5 7 9 8 6 4 2

ISBN 13: 978-1-80533-145-2

Designed and typeset by Tetragon, London
Printed and bound in the United Kingdom by Clays Ltd, Elcograf S.p.A.

www.pushkinpress.com

SPRING GARDEN

THE WOMAN was looking at something over her first-floor balcony, her hands gripping the railing, her neck craned forward.

From the ground floor, Taro watched the woman. She did not move. The sunlight that reflected off her black-framed glasses meant that Taro couldn't tell which direction she was looking, but she was faced straight ahead, towards the concrete wall and, beyond it, the house of Mrs Saeki, who owned the flats.

It was a block of flats shaped like an L flipped and rotated so that the short section was hanging down. Taro's flat was in the short section. The woman on the balcony was at the far end of the long section, the flat farthest away from his. He had happened to catch sight of her as he went to shut the small window looking out onto the courtyard—although courtyard was really too grand a word for that space, three metres wide with weeds growing in the gaps between the paving stones, and to top it all, a sign that read NO ENTRY. With the arrival of spring, the concrete wall separating the flats from Mrs Saeki's house had suddenly become thick with ivy. The two trees growing immediately behind the wall, a maple and a plum, had been left untended, and their branches now stretched over it. Behind the trees was the two-storey wooden house belonging to Mrs Saeki which, to go by its appearance, must have been pretty old. As usual, there were no signs of anyone at home.

The woman hadn't moved an inch. From where Taro stood, he could see only the concrete wall and the roof of Mrs Saeki's house, but he assumed that from the first floor the woman could probably see down to the ground level of the house and its garden. Still, what could have been so fascinating about a view like that? The most striking thing about the house's red corrugated iron roof and its dark brown wooden walls was the extent of their wear and tear. It was now a year since Mrs Saeki, who'd been living on her own, had moved into a care home for seniors. She'd looked spritely enough whenever Taro saw her sweeping the front of her house, but apparently she was about to turn eighty-six. All this Taro had learnt from the estate agent.

Beyond the roof of Mrs Saeki's house, Taro could see the sky. It had been perfectly clear when he woke up, but now there were a few clouds—bright white lumps, the sort that usually appeared in midsummer, although it was only May. Looking at the tops of the clouds that bulged right up and towered above the rest, he thought about how they actually had to be several kilometres above the earth. The contrast between them and the deep blue of the sky was so strong it hurt his eyes.

Taro imagined himself standing on a cloud. This was something he did often. After walking for miles, he would reach the cloud's edge. Grasping the edge, he would look down at the city thousands of metres below. He could see the narrow little roads intertwined, the roofs of houses clustered together. Cars the size of insects zipped along the streets. Small aeroplanes cut across the space between the city and the cloud. For some reason, in this vision of Taro's, the planes alone were cartoon drawings, nothing else. Behind their glass-fronted noses, the cockpits were empty. The planes made no sound. In fact, it wasn't just the planes that were silent—there was no noise of any kind anywhere. As Taro stood up slowly, he bumped his head up against the top of the sky. There was nobody else around.

Taro had been picturing this exact same sequence of events ever since he was a child. After it ran its course this time, he looked towards the balcony at the far end of the first floor and noticed that, all of a sudden, the scene contained a white square. Looking more closely, he saw that the woman had propped a piece of drawing paper—no, it was a sketchpad—on top of the railing. Was she drawing the trees, or what? The balcony was south-facing, and the building did not have much in the way of eaves. It was two o'clock in the afternoon. Surely too bright for sketching.

From time to time, the woman would lean her body forward to get a better view of whatever she was drawing, and Taro would get a glimpse of her face. She had shortish hair in no particular style—a fringed bob, at a stretch. Taro had seen her around after she moved into the block in February, and he guessed she was in her thirties, about the same age as he was, maybe younger. She was short, and seemingly always dressed in a T-shirt and jogging bottoms. All of a sudden, the woman lifted her neck, and her head turned in Taro's direction. Taro realized then that it wasn't Mrs Saeki's house that the woman was looking at. It was the one next to it, on the side of Taro's flat: the sky-blue house.

Right then, the sharp whistle of a bird pierced the air, and there was a rustle of leaves. In the next instant, Taro's and the woman's eyes met. Before he had time to look away, she had disappeared, taking her sketchpad with her. He heard the door to her balcony sliding shut. She didn't come out again.

■   ■   ■

When Taro came home from work on Wednesday, one of the first-floor tenants was standing at the top of the stairs outside his flat. It wasn't the woman on the balcony, but the woman from the flat next to hers. Taro guessed she was older than his mother; the woman had lived in the building for a good while.

The block of flats Taro lived in had the name View Palace Saeki III, and it was made up of eight flats: four on the ground floor, four on the first. Instead of having room numbers, the flats were identified by animals of the Chinese zodiac. So, starting with Taro's flat in the short section, the flats on the ground floor had the names Pig, Dog, Rooster, Monkey, and on the first floor, Sheep, Horse, Snake, Dragon. It was common these days for people not to put their names on the nameplates on their doors, or on their letterboxes either, so the flat names were all there was to go on. Since this woman lived in the Snake Flat, Taro thought of her as Mrs Snake. She was a friendly sort who would always strike up conversation with him whenever they ran into each other.

It was Mrs Snake who was standing at the top of the stairs, looking down to the ground floor. She calculated her timing carefully, descending just as Taro got to his door. Mrs Snake always had her hair swept up, and wore clothes of unusual cuts that could have been fashioned out of old kimonos. Today she was wearing a pair of loose-fitting, drop-crotch trousers made of fabric with a turtle pattern, together with a black shirt.

"You haven't lost your key by any chance, have you?"

"My key?" Without thinking, Taro glanced down at the key to his flat that he was holding.

"This one," Mrs Snake said, showing him a key with a mushroom-shaped key ring.

Taro recognized it immediately.

"It was lying on the ground here this morning. But you've got yours, don't you?"

"Actually, that's the key to my office. At work, I mean. I thought I had forgotten it at home. Thanks very much."

"Oh, now that's a relief! I was worried what you'd think about an old woman like me suddenly turning up with your key in my hand! I didn't want you to think I'd taken it, you know. It really was just lying right here, on the ground."

"Of course. Thank you very much."

Mrs Snake stepped towards Taro with the key, and Taro took it from her. She really was very short. She looked up at him with an almost childlike expectancy.

"So you were unable to get into work today, then?"

"Oh, no, it's not just me at the office. There are other employees at the company too."

"Ah, I see, I see. That makes sense. How stupid I am, really! I do apologize."

"No, no, not at all."

Standing there, Taro remembered the dried sardines he had in his bag. The fish, marinated in soy sauce and mirin and then dried, were a regional speciality a colleague had brought back for him from a business trip, but Taro wasn't a fan of dried fish of any kind.

He pulled out the packet and asked Mrs Snake, "Can I offer you this? It doesn't quite qualify as a thank-you present or anything, but still."

The sardines, as it turned out, were a favourite of Mrs Snake's, and she seemed genuinely delighted with the gift. So much so, in fact, that Taro felt a bit embarrassed. "Thank you so much, thank you really so much!" she said over and over, as she climbed up the stairs.

Inside his flat, Taro studied the key that Mrs Snake had returned to him. He'd bought the mushroom key ring from a vending machine. There were several different kinds of mushroom key rings dispensed at random, and all came in little plastic capsules. This one was *shimeji*. He recalled that he'd had another key ring too—in the shape of a king oyster mushroom. Taro tended to lose things, so he'd attached the mushroom key rings to his keys to make them easier to find. Maybe the king oyster mushroom key ring had got pulled off, but there was no loose metal ring or anything. He thought to himself how it might be a good idea to attach some kind of a bell to his keys so he would hear it ring when they fell.

Taro slipped the ready-made meal of chargrilled beef

and rice that he'd bought in a convenience store into the microwave, and opened a can of beer. Then stepping onto the balcony to fetch the towel drying there, he looked towards the Dragon Flat at the far end of the second floor. He could see that lights were on. It was three days since he'd seen the woman on the balcony, and he hadn't caught a glimpse of her since.

The dried sardines had been a gift from his colleague Numazu, who'd brought them back from Okayama, where he'd gone on business on Tuesday. He had taken off the Monday before to have a long weekend visiting his in-laws in Kushiro, in the east of Hokkaido, from where he'd brought back salmon jerky. Numazu had recently got married, and as his wife was an only child, he'd taken her surname as his own. It was an unusual surname that Numazu was quite fond of, and he immediately ordered a set of business cards with his new name. This was rather different from married colleagues of theirs who still used their maiden names at work. Taro hadn't got used to calling Numazu by his new name yet.

At lunch, Numazu struck up a conversation with Taro. He was totally happy about his name change, he said, but he hadn't considered the fact that adopting his wife's surname meant he would have to be buried in her family grave. He had always expected that he'd end up buried alongside his family in the port town in Shizuoka Prefecture where he'd grown up (there was a city in Shizuoka actually called Numazu, but the town that Numazu came from was not it). His family's plot was on the grounds of a temple surrounded by sloping mandarin fields that spent much of the year bathed in brilliant sunlight, so when Numazu saw his wife's family grave—in the middle of a forest that would no doubt be freezing in winter—he felt sad. "If I was a woman, I wonder if I'd find it any easier to accept being buried with the family I'd married into," Numazu said. "I can't shake the feeling that it might be pretty uncomfortable, surrounded by the remains of people I don't know."

Taro thought about this, then he said, "Things are more flexible these days. You have options about where you can get buried. Like, there are forest graveyards now, where each person has a tree instead of a gravestone, and stuff like that. In my family, we divided up my father's remains and scattered some of them."

"In that case, I want to be buried in the garden of the house where I grew up. The dog I had when I was a kid is buried there. Cheetah was his name. I'd like to be buried next to Cheetah."

Numazu then went on to tell Taro about Cheetah, a mongrel with cheetah-like black spots around his eyes that his brother had found and brought home. Cheetah loved chicken bones and would follow Numazu all the way to school. When Cheetah got older, he had problems with his hips, and couldn't be taken for walks, but still lived to a ripe old age. He'd also got much bigger than anyone imagined, and digging the hole to bury him in had been no mean feat. As Numazu rattled off this eleven-year life history in the space of five minutes, he began to tear up.

"You know," Taro said, changing the subject, "if you can make out the shape of the bones when a person is buried, it's classified as illegal disposal of a body. You have to grind the bones up into powder before you bury them, or scatter them."

"Did you?"

"It was a real struggle, actually. The bones were so hard."

"I would have thought they'd be very brittle after they came out of the oven."

Taro's father had had good, strong bones and hardly a filling in his teeth. A while back, the government had launched the 80-20 Campaign, encouraging people to live into their eighties with twenty of their real teeth intact. Taro's father had seemed like he was on target for it, but he died just before turning sixty. That was almost ten years ago. That meant it was almost ten years that Taro had been living in Tokyo.

To pulverize what was left of his father's bones, Taro had used a mortar and pestle about the size of a sugar bowl. When he moved to Tokyo from his parents' home in Osaka, he brought the mortar and pestle with him, and it was still in his flat now. Throughout the three years he'd been living with his wife—they'd divorced three years ago—the mortar and pestle had been stored in the cupboard where plates and bowls were kept. "Don't you think you should find a better place for something as precious as that?" his wife had said to him several times. "I'm going to end up using it for food one of these days." The mortar and pestle never got moved. Taro was a disorganized person, and he worried that if he moved it, he'd forget where it was. He also worried that if it wasn't somewhere visible, he would forget that his father was dead. Sometimes he got the feeling that he'd already forgotten—about his father's death, and about his existence too.

"I wonder what I should do," Numazu had gone on. "If I wait till I'm dead to think about that stuff, it'll be too late. Kushiro is so cold. It's really wild and beautiful, but it's bloody cold. I really can't stand the cold."

Taro was about to say that he wouldn't feel the cold when he was dead, but it suddenly struck him that Numazu wasn't actually wanting a conversation. He was just voicing the thoughts passing through his mind, and not looking for an answer. There were two other people in the office at that point, and they were without a doubt listening to what was being said, but neither of them uttered a word.

■　　■　　■

Taro tossed the salmon jerky from Numazu onto the shelves which had originally been for books but which now held dishes. Then, he peered around the cups and glasses on the third shelf to be sure that the mortar and pestle was still there. He'd bought it in a houseware store two days after his father died. He'd come to realize that it was a mistake to grind up his father's remains with such a thing. The mortar was lined with narrow grooves, a little too perfect for ashes to get stuck in. Taro was loath to rinse them away, though, so to this day those little furrows, like scratches made with a comb, still had some fine white powder in them. He couldn't see it, but he knew it must be there.

His father's cremated remains had been divided between the family grave in his hometown and the Buddhist altar in his mother's home. Some, which Taro had taken with him and ground up finely, had been scattered off a cape in Ehime Prefecture where his father had often gone fishing.

Carried by the wind, washed away by the waves, those finely ground ashes had soon disappeared. They had been the particles of the same bones whose powder was now stuck inside the mortar. What parts of his father were they? Taro wondered. Had those hard, white pieces of bone he'd put into the mortar really started off in his father's body? It was crazy to think that those same bones that he'd ground up in there had once been sitting around, walking about. One time, in primary school, Taro had split his forehead open on a metal pole and his classmates had all come up to him, one after another, to stare at the wound. They said you could see bone. Taro himself, though, had never got to see it. He still felt sore about that now.

The beer was too cold. Taro's refrigerator, which he'd bought second-hand, had been making funny noises recently.

On Friday morning, as Taro was about to leave for work, the woman from the Dragon Flat happened to be passing in front of the door to his flat. With her eyes fixed ahead of her, she didn't notice him. She continued walking in the opposite direction to the station. Taro paused for a moment. He couldn't have said what exactly he was thinking about or why, but he found himself following her.

The woman walked at a leisurely pace. She passed the house next to their block of flats, a building that looked like an enormous vault surrounded by exposed concrete walls, then took a right at the corner. Taro waited until she was out of sight, then approached the corner himself. The vault seemed to have a kind of courtyard within its walls, and the only windows onto the street were extremely small. He'd once caught sight of a Range Rover coming out of the garage door, now firmly shut, but had never seen any of the people who lived there.

He stopped at the corner and peered in the direction the woman had gone.

She had stopped in front of the sky-blue house, which was next to the concrete vault, and was stretching her short body as tall as it would go in an attempt to see over the wall. With her neck craned, she moved her head from side to side, then set off walking again, her eyes still focused on the sky-blue house. She was wearing a creased T-shirt and jogging bottoms, with a beanie that he guessed was to cover unkempt hair. It was not the sort of look you would go for if you were expecting to be seen by anyone. In fact, the combination of the hat and her black-framed glasses made her look pretty suspicious. She turned right again, round past the white wall.

The sky-blue house was certainly an eye-catching structure. It looked like the sort of grand, Western-style mansions that had sprung up in certain areas of Japan in the late nineteenth and early twentieth centuries. The horizontal wooden planks were painted a vivid sky blue, and the roof, tiled in terracotta, was a flattish pyramid, with a decoration at the top shaped like the tip of an arrow.

On the white wall that encircled the house, the plasterer's trowel marks formed a pattern resembling scales. From the narrow road, only the first floor of the house was visible. On the left was the balcony, and on the right were two smallish sash windows that opened vertically.

All of the window frames were painted the same colour as the terracotta roof.

The black metal entrance gates were fabricated to look like brambles, and through them Taro could see that the stained-glass window next to the front door also had a plant motif. Some kind of iris or sweet flag, in ultramarine, green and yellow. From his flat, Taro could see the part of the house on the exact opposite side of this entranceway. There was a small stained-glass window there too, with a design of red dragonflies.

The house made Taro think of the *ijinkan* in Kobe, the foreigners' mansions he'd once visited on a school trip, though in comparison, this house seemed somehow lacking in harmony. The first impression was one of taste and refinement, but the more he looked at it, the more the roof, the walls, the stained glass, the concrete wall, the gates and the windows began to seem like they'd all been gathered together from different places randomly.

To the left of the gates was a glass nameplate engraved with MORIO. Taro was under the impression that the house had been uninhabited for at least a year. When had this Morio family moved in? he wondered. A kiddie bike and a tricycle had been left by the front door. Outside the gates and to the left, parked in one of the house's two allotted spaces, was a smallish car in a shade of blue very similar to that of the house.

The garden took up about a third of the grounds of the house. It was positioned on the side facing away from his block of flats, so Taro couldn't see it from his balcony. Inside the garden, by the corner in the road, there was a large crepe myrtle tree. Even Taro could recognize it by its smooth trunk, with its patches of bark peeling off in places. A little distance away were two deciduous trees, one medium-sized and one small. Taro had passed the house only occasionally, but he somehow remembered that the crepe myrtle flowered purple, that the medium-sized tree was a white plum, and the small one appeared to be some kind of wild cherry.

When he got to the crepe myrtle, Taro stopped again, and peered around the corner where the woman had disappeared. She was already beginning to turn right by the next corner, thirty metres off. Right, right, right—in other words, she was headed back to their block of flats.

The block where Taro lived was bounded on all sides by streets so narrow that only one car could get through at a time. Looked at from above, the block was divided like a grid into four equal squares. If their block of flats was in the upper left space, then the upper right space was entirely taken up by the concrete vault, the bottom right was the Western-style sky-blue house, and the bottom left was the old wooden house belonging to Mrs Saeki.

The woman had walked a complete circle around that grid. After watching her vanish round the corner, Taro too turned right by the crepe myrtle. When he looked up at the sky-blue house, he saw that both the window that opened onto the balcony and the sash windows had their white blinds down. There was no laundry hanging on the balcony, or any drying racks either.

At the next corner, by the gate to Mrs Saeki's house, Taro checked once more to be sure of the woman's movements. He caught sight of her disappearing inside their block of flats, as he predicted. A small white van with the words DAY SERVICE printed on the side was parked in front of Mrs Saeki's house. Was she returning from the care home, or had something happened to her? He stood in that spot for a while but saw no one going in or coming out, and couldn't hear anything, so he set off walking again, not turning the corner back to the flats but heading straight, in the direction of the train station.

The next time Taro saw the woman was on Saturday, just after sundown. A slight rain was falling. The man from the Dog Flat, next to Taro's, had moved out that day, and the moving company had been there since the early morning. The flats were built of wood and offered little protection from sound, so Taro had found himself unable to take a nap while the movers were knocking around. It was just when things had finally fallen quiet, and Taro was beginning to doze off, that his intercom buzzer rang.

He could hear voices coming through the kitchen window that faced onto the outside corridor, but he picked up the phone to the intercom anyway, and heard a female voice say,

"Hello, it's me from the first floor."

Mrs Snake.

Opening the door, Taro saw that it was not just Mrs Snake, but also the Dragon Woman, standing behind her.

"Good evening!" Mrs Snake said brightly, with a big smile. Taro found himself recoiling. As usual, the Dragon Woman wore black-framed glasses and was without make-up, but today her hair was properly combed. And unlike her usual attire, the white shirt, blue cardigan and navy trousers she had on more or less constituted a matching outfit.

"This is just a little something to say thanks for the sardines," Mrs Snake said, and presented Taro with a small box wrapped in floral-patterned paper. The Dragon Woman just nodded and smiled. Looking at the two women standing there, around the same height, Taro was reminded of something, but was unsure what. Then it came to him: an old story of the stone statues of Jizō the Boddisatva that visited the house of an elderly couple who had shown them kindness, returning the favour.

Mrs Snake looked between Taro and the Dragon Woman in turn. "You know, there's only four of us left in this block! Let's not be strangers now!"

It was back in March that Taro had heard via the estate agent that Mrs Saeki had passed control of View Palace Saeki III, which had been there for thirty-one years, to her son, who had decided to demolish the building, so all residents with renewable leases were being asked to leave when their leases expired. With its cream-coloured exterior, the building didn't look as old or dishevelled as its years might have suggested, and the plumbing and utilities all worked fine, so it seemed to Taro like a waste. He even felt a bit sorry for the building, being knocked down like that when it was younger than he himself was.

Taro had moved in to the block three years ago, and had renewed his two-year lease last July, which meant he was able to stay on in his flat until July of next year.

Not all the tenants had limited-period renewable contracts like he did. Those with regular, indefinite contracts were receiving a fair sum of money as compensation for their forced eviction, and perhaps because of that, those in the Horse, Sheep and Rooster Flats had all moved out by the first week of May. The person in the Dog Flat, a grumpy-looking man with steel-rimmed glasses, had been living in the building for over ten years. When Taro had bumped into him in the corridor not long ago, the man had told him he was thinking about digging in his heels to get them to raise the compensation, but now he was gone, and without even saying goodbye.

The remaining flat, the Monkey Flat, was occupied by a young couple. Neither of them ever acknowledged Taro when they saw him, and the only thing he heard of them through the walls were their arguments.

"Oh, well, in that case, I have another packet of dried fish if you'd like."

Taro went to fetch the salmon jerky from the kitchen, but when he came back with the packet in his hand, he realized he didn't know whether he should give it to Mrs Snake or the Dragon Woman.

"Oh, I got some last week, so you take this one," Mrs Snake said to the Dragon Woman.

"Oh, thank you so much! I just love salmon jerky. It goes so well with saké, don't you think?"

The Dragon Woman's oddly animated voice went sinking into the concrete underfoot, damp with moisture from the sticky air.

"If there's anything at all I can be of help to you with, you must let me know, okay? I really mean it. Don't be shy. Promise?"

Mrs Snake went on repeating things like this, the Dragon Woman carried on smiling wordlessly, and then the two of them disappeared upstairs.

When Taro opened up the box from Mrs Snake, he found a selection of individually wrapped filter coffee sachets. They would be perfect for the office, Taro thought, and he decided to take them in the following week.

It was fifteen minutes' walk from Taro's flat to the closest train station. He regretted not choosing somewhere a bit closer, but his divorce had meant he'd had to leave his previous place in a hurry, and his search had been rushed as a result. To add to that, it had been midsummer and so hot he'd been loath to spend too much time looking. The first flat he went to see roughly met his requirements, and the rent was cheap, so he decided why not, and didn't look further. The lease was for only two years, after all, so by his thinking, once things settled down a bit in his life, he could easily move on again. But it was Taro's nature to avoid doing anything that was a bother, and he liked the Pig Flat in View Palace Saeki III well enough since it meant saving on money and effort, so when his lease expired he renewed it. Avoiding bother was Taro's governing principle. It wasn't that he was a stick-in-the-mud. It was just that, rather than putting himself out in order to get the more pleasing or interesting things he stood to gain, he always opted for the least bothersome option. Bother still seemed to find its way into his life, however.

The streets of Setagaya Ward, where he lived, were not easy to navigate. Taro had heard the story that GPS was originally invented to help people find their way around Setagaya, though he doubted it. But certainly, there was almost nowhere in the ward that formed a neat grid like the town where Taro had lived until the age of twenty-five, and there were a lot of one-way streets and dead ends. Nor was there a straight route from his flat to the station. Whichever way he took meant some circuitousness. He had three different routes he used alternately, which he'd figured out by studying the map app on his phone, and which all seemed to take about the same amount of time. When going to work, he selected one of the three routes, depending on which caught his fancy on that day.

On the third of those routes, Taro would pass a very narrow alley that ran between two houses, narrow enough that a person could touch both houses if they stretched out their arms. He'd seen someone with a Shiba go through the alley once, and decided to take the path himself. The alley was paved with concrete slabs that sloped in a V in the middle, which he knew had to be covering a culvert. He'd become interested in this kind of stuff after seeing a TV programme that traced the course of an old river that had been filled in. In this very area, in fact, there were a number of tree-lined walkways that he knew had been created by rivers having been filled in. There were other small paths that, from the snaking course you could trace on a map, were very easy to imagine as having once been streams. When Taro emerged from that narrow alley, though, the V-shaped concrete slabs also came to an end. Consulting the map, he could find no indication that there ever had been a river in that area, and concluded that the water he heard running beneath must have been sewage.

But then, a few days later, a little way from the alley, he happened upon a road going off at an odd angle from an intersection. He returned on his day off to check it out and found another alley extending diagonally from that point. It curved gently, and was dotted along both sides with old single-storey houses. The somewhat dingy alley led to a house with bags of rubbish and piles of futon in front of it. Directly across was a primary school. Crouching down, Taro could hear the sound of running water from the gutter at the side of the alley. These gutters, too, he'd become aware of from late-night TV.

Once, when he'd left the TV on past midnight, he happened to catch a programme about a person whose job was checking for leaks in underground water pipes. Using a device something like a stethoscope that he applied to the asphalt, the man listened to the sounds that could give him clues where there might be leaks. He would make his way around the residential streets in the dead of night. The footage of him filmed from behind, as he quietly went about his work while everyone was asleep, had something immensely dignified about it.

Sometimes Taro wished that he had that kind of job. He wanted to do the sort of work that drew upon a rare skill developed through experience, and that required the passion of a real artisan—a profession that wasn't much known about, but that was indispensable in sustaining people's daily lives.

Until his divorce, Taro had been a hairdresser, managing one of the branches of a hair salon owned by his wife's father. His father-in-law was a good-natured man and, saying that Taro's relationship with his daughter didn't affect his evaluation of Taro's work skills, had offered Taro a job in a branch in the neighbouring prefecture. But Taro's back pain had been getting worse, and he had grown sick of the whole lifestyle that was a part of hair salons anyway, so he was keen to be done with it. When he went home to attend the Buddhist ceremony marking the sixth anniversary of his father's death, he learnt from an old high school classmate that the Tokyo company his younger brother had started was hiring, and decided to apply.

He was now in his third year at the company, a five-person business that managed PR for other firms, and created display booths and promotional banners and signs. The job had been a total change for him, but as the manager of a hair salon, his duties had included dealing with advertising and promotion, so he wasn't a complete novice with that, and it felt fresh and exciting to have meetings with clients here and there rather than being stuck in the same space all day. So long as he did the tasks that had been assigned to him, he'd get his salary at the end of the month—which was less than before, but still. Compared to the years he'd spent staring at endless pages of monthly sales targets and customer counts while worrying about how to deal with employees and whether he was pleasing his boss, which was to say, his father-in-law, mostly going without days off, this was a piece of cake.

A little while back, during a meeting with a client who owned an imported food store and was opening a new branch, Taro discovered that the client had once lived near View Palace Saeki III.

"There's a lot of celebrities living in that area, aren't there?" the client said.

"Yes, I guess so," Taro replied.

The client mentioned a few names: an elderly stage actor who was now in suspense films on TV, an *enka* singer caught up in a debt scandal, and so on. Taro tried to seem interested.

Not long after, while taking the second of his three routes to the station, Taro discovered a house with the nameplate of one of the celebrities mentioned by the client. The actor had been the lead in a superhero series, though it was before the time when Taro had watched it. The actor's house was a three-storey affair with a façade of white tiles, its left side in the form of a half-cylinder. Looking up, Taro saw that one of its windows, curved to fit the cylindrical wall, was open, but for some reason, the house still didn't look at all like a sort of place people actually lived in. If the man himself came out at this very moment, Taro thought, I'd probably just think, well, there he is. Back when Taro was a kid, though, it would have been a different matter. He felt sure that seeing someone from TV walking around his neighbourhood, dressed totally differently from how he looked on screen, would have had a huge effect on him—he imagined it wouldn't have been joy he felt so much as confusion. Taro had liked superhero programmes when he was young, but he'd been the sort of child who'd got the most pleasure from the silly parts. He'd once made a kid at nursery cry by telling him that superheroes were just made up.

Taro had been brought up in Osaka, and to him back then, the places he saw on TV programmes seemed very far away, with no relation to the place he lived. Even the street scenes that popped up in the background looked nothing like the streets he knew, with its reclaimed land surrounded by factories. The way people spoke on TV was completely different as well—they spoke Tokyo Japanese, not Osaka dialect. For that reason, he'd been able to laugh at the programmes in safety. What would it have been like if the world from TV had actually existed in the place he'd grown up in? He'd probably have been unable to tell which version was real, and been too freaked out to leave the house. He wondered now how kids who grew up in a place like this were able to tell the difference between the two worlds.

Maybe, Taro thought to himself, maybe the person who'd moved into that sky-blue house was a celebrity too. That would mean the Dragon Woman was either a diehard fan, or else she was just a snoop. Either way, Taro thought, that would be a pretty boring solution to the mystery.

In the middle of the night, Taro was woken by the sound of a crow cawing. Wanting to keep on sleeping, he didn't open his eyes. He could hear the scratching of the crow's feet, too, and figured it must have been walking across the roof of Mrs Saeki's house. It was then he realized he needed to take his rubbish out. Funny as it was, it seemed like the crows were better at remembering the day for rubbish collection than he was. Taro had always thought crows couldn't see in the dark, though. Had they suddenly developed nocturnal vision? Were they all going around in search of that owl that had dyed the crow's wings black and fled? Wait a minute, where had he heard that story? A vague image of his classroom in nursery school floated into Taro's mind, and then he fell back into sleep.

He woke after ten o'clock, too late to take the rubbish out. He ate the bun with burdock that his boss had given him as a thank you for the coffee sachets he'd brought into work, then lay sprawled out on the tatami. Taro would always be overtaken by the urge to lie back and doze off after he'd eaten something. He'd been the same since he was a kid, and his parents had often warned him that he'd turn into a cow if he wasn't careful. As it happened, not only was Taro a Taurus, but the upper part of his head did jut out a bit at the sides, and at some point in childhood, he had genuinely believed he might become a cow. His horns, though, were yet to appear.

From time to time, Taro heard a cawing sound from the direction of Mrs Saeki's house. When crows were around making a commotion, he never heard any other bird calls. By the looks of things, it was a nice day outside. Taro could see a small section of sky through the screen door to the balcony. Viewed through the fine mesh of the screen, it looked like an image on a bad-quality monitor. Then Taro heard a noise. At first he thought it was just the wind, or another crow, or else a cat, but then he distinctly heard the scraping of stone or concrete. He stood up and walked towards the balcony, and as he got closer, he could see a human figure.

There, in the courtyard overgrown with weeds, was the Dragon Woman, in a sweatshirt and jeans, at the corner of the concrete wall that separated the courtyard from Mrs Saeki's house, the sky-blue house and the vault. She'd stacked two cement blocks, which she was using to give herself a lift as she tried to scramble up the wall. But the dense, overgrown ivy covering the wall and the maple branches poking over the top weren't making it easy. Her feet searched around in vain for a foothold.

"Hey!" Taro called out from his balcony.

The Dragon Woman turned around.

"I don't think you're supposed to be there."

The woman stared blankly at Taro for a few seconds, then suddenly shot him a friendly smile.

"You're absolutely right!"

She came over to stand next to his balcony.

"I wonder, then, could I possibly trouble you for a favour?"

Here we go, thought Taro to himself. This is where the trouble begins. These kinds of favours that people asked were never good news. They were phrased like polite questions, but he was never really being given an option.

"I just really want to take a look at that house. There's something I want to check out."

The Dragon Woman stretched her finger towards the sky-blue house that lay beyond the ivy-covered wall. Taro didn't say anything, and looked in the direction she was pointing.

"I was wondering if you wouldn't mind me getting up on your balcony railing. I think the best view of all would be from the flat above yours, but the person in there has already moved out. I'm not up to anything bad, I promise. I'm not planning a break-in, and I'm not going to take sneaky photos or anything like that. It's just that I, well, I really like it. The house, I mean."

The house. Taro turned to look at it now. The light blue walls, the terracotta tiled roof. He could hear a bird chirping, but could see no sign of it.

"It's private property, you know."

"I'm really not up to anything underhanded, I promise. It's just such a wonderful building. I'm an artist, I mean, that's my job, and there's something I want to check out. For my drawings."

"For your drawings."

"I promise I won't cause you any trouble."

"Okay," Taro said. He found these kinds of conversations a real pain. He could see that giving in to the woman now would most likely lead to greater trouble in the future, but his tendency was to do anything he could to avert the bother that lay immediately in front of him. As it happened, that personality trait was one of the reasons his ex-wife had given for wanting a divorce.

The Dragon Woman thanked him, then brought over the two blocks she'd been using before, placed them at the foot of his balcony, and began to climb up. Making it clear he wanted nothing to do with the whole thing, Taro went back inside his flat and stood a step away from the balcony. He'd thought the Dragon Woman was about the same age as he was, a little over thirty, but close up in broad daylight, her face looked tired and somehow lacking youth, and he suddenly wondered if she was a fair bit older. It was the sort of face that made it impossible to judge her age with any accuracy, though. He could have heard she was forty and accepted it as the truth as readily as he would if he heard she was still in high school. On that unmade-up face, her black-framed glasses stood out even more.

"That window is where the landing is, on the stairs."

The Dragon Woman was sitting on the railing of his balcony and was pointing again in the direction of the sky-blue house. There was a small stained-glass window, with a design of two red dragonflies, exactly halfway between the ground and first floors. Taro had the feeling he'd seen that window lit up from the inside quite recently, but he didn't have a clear memory of when it had been. The Dragon Woman got herself to the corner of the railing, placed her hands against the wall, then carefully stood up. From that position, she pointed to somewhere beyond where the sky-blue house met the concrete vault house. Taro stepped out once more onto the balcony and peered in that direction, but it was too dim to see anything clearly.

"That window down there must be the bathroom window. But you can't see as well from here as I thought. Sorry for the imposition," the Dragon Woman said, then clambered down from the railing and set her feet on Taro's balcony.

"Well, hello!" Taro heard a voice say from above. He looked up to see Mrs Snake leaning over the top of her balcony towards them. She smiled meaningfully and bowed, then stayed put, looking down at them. When Taro bowed back in her direction, she disappeared from the balcony edge.

The Dragon Woman's face registered no particular emotion. She brushed away the dust on her hands and knees, then, taking off her trainers and holding them in one hand, entered Taro's flat without the least hesitation. "Is it okay to go out through the front door?" she asked.

Then she added, "The high school I went to was next to a police station, and if one of the policemen ever saw a girl and a boy alone together in one of the classrooms, they'd call up the staff of the school right away. Can you believe that? I think they must have had overactive imaginations."

Taro had no idea why she would come out with that kind of thing in this situation, but he didn't want there to be silence between them, so he said, "How old do you think Mrs Snake is?"

"Mrs Snake?"

"The woman in the Snake Flat."

"Ah, I get it!"

The Dragon Woman told Taro both Mrs Snake's age and her real name, and also that Mrs Snake was a Scorpio. Taro found the name unexpected, somehow, and felt that Mrs Snake suited her much better. Hearing her age, Taro determined right away that she had been born in the same year as his father. It was the year that the Second World War had ended, so come the summer, the number of years that had elapsed since then would pop up here and there in the media. Since Taro's father had died of a subarachnoid haemorrhage, those figures that appeared in the media each year had been the age he would have been if he'd still been alive. Taro's mother was exactly ten years younger than that, but she'd soon overtake the age his father had reached. His father's birthday was February, which meant, if she were a Scorpio, Mrs Snake had been born nine months after him. But his father's age would now never go beyond fifty-nine. During his father's life, Taro had just assumed that his father would go on to become elderly, but now he couldn't imagine his father as a typical old man at all. A vision of the mortar and pestle in his kitchen cabinet came to mind. Now, that was the closest thing to his father that he had, at least here in Tokyo, and yet his father hadn't even known of its existence.

"In that case, my flat should have been on the ground floor. My surname's Nishi, and my kanji looks a lot like the kanji for the Rooster. It would have been easy to remember me that way, right?"

"Hmm."

"This flat has a different layout from the others. I was thinking this is how it might be. Is the bathroom on this side?"

Carrying her trainers, Nishi walked slowly towards the front door, looking around her as she went. Taro ended up following behind.

"I think the floor area itself is the same."

Taro's Pig Flat in the protruding section of the building was longer and narrower than the flats in the block's main section, but all of the flats were the same in that they had kitchens of ten square metres, tatami rooms of just over thirteen square metres, and a separate bath and toilet.

"This layout feels more spacious somehow, though. A kitchen facing this way seems like it'd be easier to use, too."

"Really?"

"I think so."

Apparently satisfied with her investigation of the flat, Nishi stood in the entranceway and slipped on her shoes. Then she said, "Can I buy you dinner as a thank you for this?"

Nishi and Taro walked to a restaurant on the other side of the level crossing, one station away from the station where Taro caught his train every day. It was a small station and express trains didn't stop there, only local trains, so Taro had never had reason to set foot there before.

Nishi told him that the restaurant's deep-fried foods were a speciality. It was hard to say which was better, she said—the octopus or the chicken. They ordered a plate of each, and two beers.

Sitting opposite Nishi, Taro realized that although the paleness of the skin on her face suggested she rarely went outside, she was surprisingly muscular. The arms and neck emerging from her T-shirt were well toned, and looked like they'd be firm to the touch.

When he asked if she'd used to play some kind of sport when she was younger, she answered, unexpectedly, yes, she'd played baseball. It was only when she was in primary school, though, she said, and she'd never actually taken part in games, just practised. Nishi polished off her first beer before the food had arrived, and ordered another straight away.

Then she brought out a bag made of fabric with a beetle pattern, and removed a book from it.

"This book is that house," she said.

It was a large, thin book with the title *Spring Garden*. Each page contained four to six photographs, much like a family album. They were mostly black-and-white.

"See? It is, right?"

Nishi opened the book to a page with a photo of the house's exterior. It was one of just a handful of colour shots. With its sky-blue wooden walls, terracotta roof tiles, and the pointed decoration at the very top, there was no doubting it was that house. The photograph had been taken from the garden, and it was the first time that Taro saw the ground floor of the house on that side. There was a large sunroom, with sliding glass doors to the outside.

"Whoa," Taro said, peering at the photograph across the table, "the interior is all Japanese style."

Most of the ground floor was taken up by large tatami rooms, linked by sliding Japanese-style doors. A woman was sitting on one of the large wicker chairs in the sunroom, smiling broadly. She was young, with short hair. The photograph next to it showed a slender, long-haired man in a white shirt, standing in front of a Japanese dresser in one of the ground-floor rooms. The dresser was an impressive multi-compartment affair with embossed black iron fixtures, the kind that you saw in antique shops.

"Yes. It's got a totally different feel from the outside, hasn't it? See the design on those wooden panels above the sliding doors? It's elephants. I'm not sure if they were aiming for an Indian look or what."

The wooden panels she was speaking of were above the lintel to the doors separating the two tatami rooms. The short-haired woman had grabbed onto that lintel and was swinging from it, laughing. There was a photograph of the dragonfly stained-glass panel that Taro could see from his window, too. Just as Nishi had said before, it was positioned on the landing, midway up the stairs. In the picture, the slender, long-haired man was standing on the landing, peering into an old twin-lens reflex camera.

Both the room leading to the first-floor balcony and the one with the Western-style sash windows had tatami floors. Beneath one of the sash windows was a writing desk. The woman was standing in front of it, holding a cushion as if she were about to throw it at the camera.

"It was built in 1964, the same year as the Tokyo Olympics. It's totally got that look of the sort of house 'a person of culture' around that time would have built, but it seems a bit lacking in taste now, the way they've crammed so many different elements in."

"I know what you mean."

Of the ten or so colour photos, there was one of the garden as seen from the sunroom: to the left, back by the wall, was the crepe myrtle; to its right, the tree that looked like a wild cherry; and further right, the plum. All of that was just the same as Taro had observed from the road the other day, but in front of the plum in the photograph was a stately pine tree. Beneath it, stones had been arranged to create the effect of a stream, and there was also a small stone lantern. The centre pages featured two large photographs with a very similar composition, showing almost the entirety of the garden. The photo on the right showed the woman standing on the lawn, and in the photo on the left, the slender, long-haired man was standing in exactly the same spot. In both the photos, it was spring. The branches of the plum tree, even sparser then than they were now, were covered in lustrous green leaves, and the tree to its left, still relatively low to the ground, was covered in flowers that looked like cherry blossoms, though in brighter pink. The crepe myrtle was also a bit shorter than it was now. Its leaves had begun to come out, but it wasn't yet in bud. There were a few small white flowers dotting the ground as well.

On the last page of the book was a single colour photograph, about eight-by-twelve centimetres, surrounded by a thick border of white. It showed the bathroom. The walls and the floor were covered in tiny tiles in varying shades of green. The effect was like a mosaic, perhaps of trees, or waves. There was no one in the photo, neither the woman nor the man, and the bathtub was empty. The light filtering through the small window gently lit up the green space.

"Isn't the bathroom just great? That's my favourite photo in the whole book. There's something about those lime-green tiles."

Then Nishi began to tell Taro the story of how she'd come to know about the house. While browsing estate sites online in search of a place to live, she'd got hooked on photos of the many grand mansion-style houses in Setagaya. So when she came upon the photo of this house, with its unusual sky-blue exterior, she'd recognized it immediately. Nishi then searched online for the book of photos and, from the various volumes on offer second-hand, selected the one listed AS NEW and clicked BUY NOW, even though it cost a bit more than the others. Three days later, *Spring Garden* arrived in the post. It had been published two decades earlier, but the book was in almost pristine condition. Apart from a few light scratches on the front cover, there was no damage, and it hadn't faded at all. It was as though it had been sleeping all those years in some kind of warehouse. In fact, it looked like it could have been published yesterday. And yet, it was a photograph collection documenting the everyday life of a married couple living in that particular house twenty years ago: the husband, a thirty-five-year-old director of TV commercials, and the wife, a twenty-seven-year-old actress in a small theatre company.

It was clear that the house had undergone change since the book was published, but it didn't matter. Nishi saved each of the images of the sky-blue house from the site onto her smartphone, so that she could look at the snaps of the structure and its floor plan whenever she felt like it: The ground floor was the front entrance with its stained glass, the forty-square-metre living room, the sunroom, the kitchen fitted out in plain wood, and the bathroom, while the first floor had the two Western-style rooms of ten square metres, a slightly larger tatami room of thirteen square metres and the balcony. Then, of course, there was the garden with the crepe myrtle, the plum and the Hall crabapple.

As enamoured of the house as she was, Nishi wasn't able to move into it. A three-bedroom house of that size was too big for a single person, and the rent was a staggering 300,000 yen per month. But there was a flat for rent directly behind it that otherwise fulfilled her requirements exactly, and it was good to have something close by like that to bring a bit of excitement to your day-to-day. In fact, Nishi said, she had believed since childhood that she had luck on her side.

If she loved the house so much, though, Taro asked, had she not even requested that the estate agent show it to her? And had she not considered the possibility of living there with someone else and sharing the rent? Nishi said that was out of the question: she found it impossible to relax when there was something moving in her space. She also explained that her conscience, which was unbending in certain areas, wouldn't allow her to bother an estate agent when she had no intention of renting the house. What was more, she certainly didn't look like the sort of person who could afford it. One time in the past, when she'd gone to look at a place that was just slightly above her price range, the landlady told her that it was clearly not the sort of place for a person like her, Nishi told Taro, then cackled.

So that was how Nishi had come to live on the first floor of View Palace Saeki III, a thirty-one-year-old building, fifteen minutes' walk to the train station. The lease was for two years, and when told about the owner's plans to demolish the building, she replied that she didn't mind. She moved in at the start of February.

Nishi had been living in Tokyo for twenty years now, and that had been her fourth move within the city.

When she was younger, she'd lived in an enormous housing estate in Nagoya, close to the industrial belt by the coast. On the northern side of the estate were the municipally run low-income housing blocks, and on the southern side were those run by public corporations. Nishi lived with her parents and younger brother in a block in the middle of the twelve municipal towers, a flat on the third floor of a four-storey building. Outside the window stood rows of four-storey buildings identical to hers. When she went over to the flats of friends at the local school, which had been built at the same time as the estate, each and every one of them was laid out in the same way. She felt a vague yearning for the sorts of houses she saw on TV or in comics, with flights of stairs or hallways in them. Or maybe it wasn't exactly a yearning—maybe it was more that she was fascinated by them. She wanted to know what it would feel like to live in a house that had stairs in it, and hallways, and wondered too about the kinds of people who would live in those kinds of houses. She even went through a phase of collecting estate agency flyers, and she and her friends would sketch floor plans of their ideal houses and compare their ideas. Sometimes they would decide which room they would have for their own and which would belong to the other members of the family, and then have imaginary conversations based on those scenarios, like a slightly more grown-up version of playing house.

At around the age of fifteen, Nishi's family moved to Shizuoka Prefecture, not far from Tokyo. The estate this time had only four tower blocks, but their new flat was on the third floor of a four-storey building that was strikingly similar to their previous one—right down to the layout of the rooms—so there wasn't any need to rethink the positioning of the furniture. The surroundings weren't much different either. There were factories and warehouses lining the coast, and highways circling the town. Nishi bicycled to school alongside wide dusty roads with lorries coming and going beside her.

Her first encounter with *Spring Garden* took place in the classroom at lunchtime, in her final year of high school. One of her friends had brought the book to school, though she couldn't recall who. Books of photographs weren't popular in the way they would later go on to be, but some authors and actresses popular at the time had praised this one, and it was written up in various culture magazines, making it something of a hit. Going on that, it seemed likely that either Kobayashi, who was in a band, or Nakamura, who was hoping to go to art school, brought the book to school. All Nishi could remember for certain, though, was that someone opened up the book when they were crowded round a desk eating their bento box lunches and one of Takahashi's cherry tomatoes rolled across its open pages.

The book was a collaboration between Taro Gyushima, an advertising director, and his wife, Kaiko Umamura, a stage actress. About two-thirds of the photos had been taken by Gyushima, the rest by Kaiko.

At that time, several of Taro Gyushima's TV adverts were the talk of the town, and there would often be interviews with him in magazines. One of his adverts featured actresses whose bodies looked like they were made of porcelain or metal, as if rendered with computer graphics, and another depicted in soap-opera style a highly detailed imaginary world inhabited by a made-up race of people. The adverts really were unlike anything that had come before, and spawned many imitations, but they struck Nishi as too contrived, and she wasn't a fan.

The photographs that made up *Spring Garden*, on the other hand, were mostly regular shots, and unlike the commercials, seemed pretty unpretentious. Nishi thought it a really good collection of photos. She liked the innocent look that Kaiko Umamura had about her, and found her handstands, cartwheels and various other odd poses fun. There were even shots of the actress brushing her teeth in the garden, and taking a nap at the low table.

Nishi studied the house where the couple lived in great detail. It was a world apart from the standardized accommodation that she had grown up in. The stained glass and the carved panels above the doors looked custom-made. Even the handrail on the stairs had carvings in it. From watching television and reading comics, Nishi was familiar with things like windows that opened up and down in the Western style instead of side to side like the old Japanese ones, not to mention sunrooms and gardens, but they had never made an appearance in her own life. Best of all, though, she liked the bathroom with its mosaic of tiles in that mysterious pattern. It reminded her of a photo she'd seen of the walls in a block of flats designed by Gaudi. Of course, the bathroom in the sky-blue house wasn't in quite such good taste, but the thought that there were people who had specifically commissioned a bathroom like that, people who had built it, and people who used that bathtub day in day out, brought a smile to her face.

It was while looking at that book that it occurred to Nishi for the first time that maybe falling in love and getting married and all that stuff might not actually be such a bad thing. In the photographs, Taro Gyushima and Kaiko Umamura seemed totally content. Never before or since had Nishi felt such a strong sense that living with someone you loved could be enjoyable. Six months later, she enrolled in university in Tokyo where, at the suggestion of a girl she sat next to in the matriculation ceremony, she joined the university's photography club. *Spring Garden* was on the bookshelf of the clubroom, and Nishi would often take it down and flip through it. She didn't buy a copy herself because she was spending a lot of money as it was on cameras and film and supplies, and she could look through the book whenever she wanted at the clubroom. When she graduated, and no longer had access to a darkroom, she more or less stopped taking photographs. What Nishi had liked best of all were those moments in the darkroom when she would stand in front of a piece of photographic paper dipped in developer and watch as a scene straight out of the past came floating to the surface. Without those moments, she hadn't much use for photography at all.

Nishi stayed on in Tokyo after graduating. The first place she lived in by herself was an old flat in the suburbs. The block of flats was built on the same grounds as the landlord's house, and the window of her first-floor flat had a great view over the trees into the landlord's large garden. From there, Nishi would watch the seasons changing. The Hall crabapple blossomed, then the zelkova would come into bud, the hydrangea would change colour, the crepe myrtle would shed its flowers for a good three months, and the bright orange flowers of the osmanthus would infuse the garden with its scent, then the leaves would turn and fall. In February, when the weather was still cold, she would catch a whiff of something and discover the vivid pink of the plum tree in bloom, and not long after that the big white magnolia flowers would open. The magnolia and the Hall crabapple she found particularly beautiful.

Up until that point, Nishi had always thought of trees as something that grew by the road or in parks, or else up in the mountains far away, so being able to watch the seasons passing like that from inside her own home came as a real surprise. What was more, the garden wasn't visible from the road, so they were seasons shared only by the landlord's family and the people living in her block. The plants in the garden weren't just objects that grew older with the passing years, she realized. Rather, they grew and they blossomed, and new buds appeared on branches that had dried up during the winter. There was life, plenty of it. Nishi had never had a pet of any kind, and the fact that there were living things that had no connection to her, inhabiting the same space as her, seemed wondrous.

That landlord's house was gone now, destroyed in a fire. It happened after Nishi had moved out, and fortunately, there had been no casualties. The house had looked a lot like Mrs Saeki's, next to View Palace Saeki III. That fact made Nishi suspect that her selection of her current flat wasn't a complete coincidence.

Spring Garden, which could not now be found in bookshops anywhere, was supposedly a collaboration between Taro Gyushima and Kaiko Umamura, but there was no indication which photos had been taken by whom. The book was the only photo collection that either of them had made. Two years after its publication, the couple divorced. Taro Gyushima became an artist and moved to Berlin. Very occasionally, his name would appear in flyers or announcements for art-related events in Japan, even now. And Kaiko Umamura gave up her acting career. She had never been a major actress to begin with—number three even within her small company, plus the occasional bit-part in films—so it was little wonder that she had disappeared without trace.

In one photo, where sunlight from the window reached a good distance onto the tatami, Kaiko Umamura was right in the middle of it, doing a handstand. Even without a wall for support, her legs were entirely straight, her toes pointed. She must have been an exceptionally sporty type. One of Nishi's university friends who went to a lot of theatre had told her Umamura often did backwards somersaults in the swordfights of the plays she performed in.

One photo showed a birdcage hanging in the sunroom. Sunlight was coming from behind it, and that part of the photo looked to be deliberately out of focus, so it was hard to know what was in the cage, but it looked like some kind of parrot or parakeet. Who had taken the bird after the divorce? Nishi wondered to herself, and then concluded that it must have been Kaiko. It must have been Kaiko who named it as well. She'd read an article online about how Winston Churchill's parrot was still alive, so it was highly possible that the bird was still living with Kaiko somewhere now.

When Nishi first moved into her current flat in February, the trees in Mrs Saeki's garden had been mostly bare, but there were still a lot of birds that came flying through the cold air to perch on them. The electronic dictionary Nishi owned included an *Illustrated Guide to Birds* among its additional features, and she used the photos and recordings of the bird calls to identify the birds that appeared in the garden: brown-eared bulbuls, Oriental turtle doves, sparrows, tits, azure-winged magpies, and so on. The brown-eared bulbul was described in the *Illustrated Guide* as having a 'loud and nagging' call. She looked it up in a guidebook to wild birds, and learnt that it only existed in Japan and nearby countries, meaning that in the rest of the world it was thought of as a pretty rare species.

Nishi often went out on the balcony of the Dragon Flat with her ring-bound sketchbook to draw the plants that appeared in Mrs Saeki's garden as the seasons changed, or the cats that went walking along the top of the concrete wall, or the roofs and windows of the houses, and even sometimes the passing butterflies.

Nishi worked as an illustrator and a comic-strip artist. After graduating from university, she was employed by a company that did contract work for an advertising agency. While working there, she had begun to take on illustration jobs on the side, and had quit her job five years ago when a manga series she'd written was given a weekly slot in a magazine. Now, her main jobs were making comic strips out of readers' stories submitted to a job-seeking portal and a cooking magazine site, and individual commissions for magazines and adverts. On her homepage, she occasionally posted short comic strips based on Chinese legends or idioms that came from particular historical events.

In March, she had met with an editor who had suggested collecting these pieces together and publishing them as a book. At that time, the editor had mentioned in passing a proposal he'd made for a book of photos, rejected on the grounds that books of photos didn't sell these days, which had prompted Nishi to raise the topic of *Spring Garden*. But the editor in question, still in his mid-twenties, had heard neither of the book itself nor of Taro Gyushima or Kaiko Umamura, and hadn't seemed particularly interested. A few days later, though, when stuck for conversation with his boss, the editor had suddenly remembered that her previous job had been something to do with theatre and the arts, and he had asked on a whim if she had heard of Taro Gyushima or Kaiko Umamura. As it happened, his boss had interviewed Kaiko Umamura several times while working for an events magazine. She reminisced to the editor about how she had gone to an after-party for a show, and how, following that, Kaiko Umamura had given her a collection of annotated illustrations that she'd produced after her divorce. The editor, getting excited and declaring this an amazing example of synchronicity, told his boss about how Nishi was a huge fan of Kaiko Umamura's. The boss thought he was using the word 'synchronicity' wrong, but nevertheless, heartened by the fact that this subordinate of hers she found difficult to relate to was listening to her with apparent interest for once, hunted down the collection of illustrations and brought it in. A few days later, it was delivered to Nishi in a padded envelope.

Made of A4-sized paper folded in half and stapled together, the pamphlet Nishi received was less like a book of illustrations, and more like a handmade zine. It had eighteen pages, colour-photocopied rather than printed. Tiny illustrations in colour pencil, about the size of postage stamps, were scattered randomly across the pages. There was the stained-glass window with the red dragonflies, a wicker chair, the sunroom, various bits of tableware. It seemed like the illustrations were all either parts of the sky-blue house or objects she'd used in there. They were really no more than doodles, but assured doodles nonetheless, that captured the shape of what they were depicting very well. Short writings snaked their way between them.

Wooden houses sure let the cold in! Brrr!
Found a caterpillar on the porch. I really hate insects.
Why does it have to be dragonflies? Insects are gross...
Been studying the strips of fabric round the edge of the
tatami mats. The patterns are different on the ground
floor and first floors. Something about staring at those
nothingy patterns makes me remember being little.
I like this window. The glass is a little bit warped, and
it makes it seem like the air outside is warped too. The
light bends, changes speed.
I'm soooo sleepy...

Broke a teacup. The thought of sweeping it up and throwing it away made me too sad so I just left it there.

It was mostly jottings, like talking to herself, but through the medium of pen and paper. There was no mention of Taro Gyushima, nor of any of her plays or her friends or anything like that. The booklet was about bits of the house and her thoughts about them.

Nishi was impressed by how good the drawings were. The jottings weren't fascinating or anything like that, but they seemed exactly like the things that she would have expected the Kaiko Umamura who appeared in that book of photos to say. It came to Nishi that the captions might work perfectly as speech bubbles, so she photocopied the booklet, cut out the lines of text, and tried arranging them on top of the photos.

A few days later Nishi received an email from the same editor, saying that his boss had learnt that Kaiko Umamura was now running a yoga school. He included a link to the yoga school's website. If it was just a regular yoga school, Nishi thought, then maybe she could go and actually meet Kaiko Umamura in the flesh. With anticipation and a fair amount of apprehension, Nishi clicked on the link to the homepage.

The site that appeared on Nishi's computer screen was simple and tasteful. The top page showed a picture of a woman holding a yoga pose in a forest of bright green leaves. Her head was turned to the side, and the light was coming from behind it, so it was impossible to make out her expression. When Nishi scrolled down to look at the address of the school, she saw it was in Yamanashi Prefecture, just outside of Tokyo, in one of the cooler regions that people often went to escape the summer heat. Nishi clicked on the tab that read ABOUT THE INSTRUCTOR, and a photograph of a woman appeared, and beside it the name ASUKA SAWADA. Apparently, that was Kaiko Umamura's real name.

The first thought that came to Nishi's mind was that the woman was stunning. In that yoga pose, with her long black hair swept up into a ponytail, Asuka Sawada definitely resembled Kaiko Umamura. The long, narrow eyes and large mouth were the same. The pose she was adopting too, with her back arched, recalled her acrobatics on the pages of *Spring Garden*.

And yet, Nishi could not but feel that the woman in those photos was not, in fact, Kaiko Umamura. Her INSTRUCTOR'S MESSAGE, full of wholesome words like 'natural power', 'purification', and 'betterment', didn't square up with the woman whose face beamed out of the book of photos, or with the one who'd put together that collection of illustrations. Nishi looked through the back entries of the blog that was linked on the website, but the more she read, the further Asuka Sawada grew apart from Kaiko Umamura.

Nishi closed the web page and opened up *Spring Garden*. Seeing Kaiko Umamura there, she felt a surge of relief. When she stepped out onto her balcony, there was the sky-blue house, unchanged, bathed in sunlight. Inside that house were the windows and stairs that Kaiko Umamura had drawn, Nishi thought, and the desire to make sure of that fact for herself, just once, rose up in her.

Nishi walked past the house twice a day, and gazed out at it from the balcony of the Dragon Flat. The advert for it disappeared from the estate agency site in the middle of February, but there was no sign of anyone moving in, so she guessed that something must have made them decide not to rent it out after all.

It was perhaps this reasoning that made her careless. In any case, to her great frustration, Nishi had been out on the day when the new people moved in, and she had missed it. At the end of March, she had gone for a couple of days to visit her mother, who lived in Chiba Prefecture. Heading out on her morning walk around the block as usual on the day after she got back, and seeing a small car parked in front of the sky-blue house and a tricycle inside the gates, Nishi felt genuine shock. Approaching the gates, she saw there was already a nameplate reading MORIO, and when she looked up she saw a white blind drawn in one of the first-floor windows.

TOMOKA SHIBASAKI

No, Nishi thought to herself. That's not how it is in *Spring Garden*. There was now a blind in the window where there was supposed to be curtains, a tricycle and a bike and various kids' toys lying outside the front door as if it was the most normal thing in the world, and a nameplate with a modern-looking font.

Nishi's insides were all in commotion. She returned to her flat, but could hardly concentrate on her work at all. That day, she walked by the house every hour. At four in the afternoon, she saw the car that had vanished at one o'clock returning. Concealing herself behind a telegraph pole, Nishi saw a young-looking mother with two young children getting out of the car. The boy looked about five, and the little girl was in her mother's arms.

Nishi found the idea that people really had begun living in the house unsettling, somehow bewildering. At first, she thought those feelings were driven by a sense of danger—danger that the house was now going to change and become different from the way it was in the photo book—but after a week of walking past the house that was so rapidly adjusting to its role as the Morio family residence, she realized that that wasn't it.

Time, which had stopped while the house was empty, was now moving again. The structure itself was exactly the same as it had been a week ago when nobody was in it, and yet its colours, the feel of the place, were now wholly different. It wasn't just that people were living in it—it was that the house itself had suddenly come back to life. The house which Nishi had been convinced she could carry on looking at forever, in the same way as she could the house in the photos, felt now as if it had taken on a mind of its own, and begun moving. As dramatic as it sounded, it honestly seemed that the house had taken on the same quality as a doll that had suddenly become human. Every time she passed by the house, every time she saw the envelopes poking out from the letterbox or the sheets hanging out to dry on the balcony, she had the physical sensation like something rubbing at her body from the inside.

Since that first day, she had caught sight of the Morios several times. Both of the children got on the same bus that took them to nursery school. It seemed as though the father was usually late getting home, but on one occasion she spotted him. He was a tall man who looked very elegant in his black suit.

Nishi felt closer to the sky-blue house now that it had people living in it, but by the same token, it had also become someone else's, and therefore a place that she wasn't allowed to enter. Thinking that she wasn't allowed in made her want to see it all the more.

If she could somehow get to know Mrs Morio, she thought, then she might be able to find an excuse to enter, so she racked her brains for some way that she might make her acquaintance, but the sorts of places they went and their ways of life were so different as to make it seem impossible. Surely, she told herself, there must be a way.

During the period that she told Taro all this, Nishi polished off seven beers, and went to the ladies' twice. Taro switched to oolong tea after his first beer. Since his divorce, he'd made it a rule for himself to never drink more than one beer, and had stuck to it now for three years.

Sometimes even now, the image of his dad tripping and falling while drunk at home would flash through Taro's mind. At first, his dad had only drunk beer, but then at some point—Taro didn't remember exactly when—had progressed to *shochu*, and from one glass to two, and then three. If he'd lived longer, he would no doubt have gone on to drink more and more.

Nishi now took a sip from her eighth beer, then looked unflinchingly at Taro from behind her black-rimmed glasses.

"There's something that's been bothering me for a long time."

Her eyes look drunk, Taro thought.

"What's with the rat and the ox and stuff?"

"The rat?..."

"The names of the flats, I'm talking about. They start with Dragon, right? That's the fifth one in the zodiac. That means the first four are missing. I think there must have been a View Palace Saeki I and II."

"I guess that would make sense."

"I walked around the area a lot looking for them but with no luck. I asked the estate agent too, and they said they had no idea."

"They've probably been demolished already."

"Right! That's what I was thinking too. But we're talking just the first four, right? Rat, Ox, Tiger, Rabbit. It's hard to imagine two buildings with just two flats each. Or else, maybe there's some kind of hidden meaning to it all."

"Who knows."

Taro lifted his glass of oolong tea, but it was now only ice. The food had been just as good as it had been billed to be. Taro felt like he marginally preferred the deep-fried chicken over the octopus.

"I'm really sorry. When I get nervous I always talk too much to try and cover it up."

Nishi shot him a grin as she drained the last of her eighth beer. Glancing at her in profile, Taro said, "I think you must be about the same age as my older sister."

"Really? I've got a younger brother too, actually, a year younger. What does your sister do?"

"She works in a college in Nagoya."

"In Nagoya! Whereabouts?"

"Where was it again? I've forgotten the name of the place."

"Ask her next time, and tell me! Do you look alike?"

"People don't seem to think so. We're five years apart, after all, and kind of different. She works all year round and saves up for a big annual holiday overseas. She's just come back recently from—ah, where was it? Some kind of ruins in Mexico."

"Wow, she sounds interesting. Does she ever come to Tokyo?"

"Not at all, no. I haven't seen her in three years."

"Three years! Wow."

"Yeah, that's how it is with us. We sometimes email each other and stuff, but that's about it."

"Really! Wow, gosh, I can't imagine. Wow."

Nishi had suddenly become very friendly, no doubt owing to the drink. But Taro decided that stoking her enthusiasm further would only mean bother, so he resisted telling her that he shared a first name with the guy who'd lived in the sky-blue house, or that he'd grown up in a municipal estate like she had. It hadn't been a four-storey one, but a fourteen-storey one—cutting-edge, at the time it had been built. Taro's flat had been on the twelfth floor. He had slept in a bunk bed by the window that led onto the balcony, and from the time he'd started school, the bottom bunk had been his sister's, and the top bunk his. Every night, before going to sleep, he had looked out at the city. There was the bridge going over the canal, the factories with their bare metal scaffolding, and the chimneys rising above the rubbish-incineration plant. The incineration plant had flashing red lights, and when he breathed in and out three times in time with them, he would get sleepy. That was something his sister had taught him.

The restaurant bill was so cheap that Taro wondered if there wasn't some kind of mistake. Nishi paid, as she'd promised. As they headed towards the station, she announced that she was going to visit a friend. Taro accompanied her as far as the ticket gates, where Nishi removed her copy of *Spring Garden* from the cloth bag, and split it into two—or so it seemed until Taro figured out that there had been two books all along. Nishi held one of them out to him.

"I was in such a rush to get it I ended up ordering two copies. So here, you have one."

Taro accepted his copy of the book and thanked her. Then holding it in one hand, he wandered towards View Palace Saeki III. When he passed the shopping arcade and found himself on the residential streets, everything around him was dark and quiet, and he didn't see a soul.

Taro thought about how different the place he now lived was from the place he'd grown up—the size of the buildings and the gaps between them, the number of people living there, the general feel of it, everything. His home town as it existed in his memory seemed distant to him, like something that belonged to another person. It was almost as though he'd mistaken a place he'd seen on TV or in a film for a thing of his own, or else that the sights seen by someone in one of the thousand or so different flats on that estate had somehow snuck their way into his mind and still remained there. That was how it seemed from time to time.

The next morning, when Taro opened his door, he found a paper bag, inside of which was a twenty-centimetre-square cardboard box and a slip of paper with a note in green ink:

My friend's gift shop is closing down, so she gave me this. It's a cuckoo clock. I thought I'd give it to you as a thank-you present. Nishi.

Taro found it hard to see appeal in anything that made a noise every hour. He lifted the lid of the box just far enough to glimpse the wooden top of the clock, then closed it again immediately, and put it away inside his closet.

At some point not long after that, Taro began to pass along the side of the Morios' house on his way to work. It was a little bit of a detour for him, but not too much.

Occasionally there would be a German car parked in front of the house, alongside the small family car. He'd heard from Nishi that the husband drove this second car to work. It was dark navy, an unusual sort of colour for a car. The walls of the house and the second car were both a light shade of blue, so Taro assumed that at least someone in the family must be keen on the colour.

Sometimes he would hear high-pitched children's voices, but he had never actually seen the Morio kids. He felt sure that Nishi, passing by the house several times a day as she did, would come to be known to the inhabitants as someone to watch out for, if in fact that hadn't happened already.

After a few days, Taro noticed it wasn't just the Morios' house that he was examining carefully, but all the houses on his way to work.

Taro's immediate neighbourhood was said to be a posh part of town, but it wasn't as though the posh and less posh parts of town were divided up by street, or anything so obvious. To be sure, there was a kind of slow shift taking place, so the large houses and low-rise blocks of high-class flats gradually gave way to more blocks of single-room flats, narrow houses, and multi-purpose buildings with restaurants, shops and offices the closer you got towards the station. Still, there were places where a block of flats older and more cramped than View Palace Saeki III stood right next to a great big detached house with security cameras affixed to the walls, and at the end of an alley off the shopping arcade that led up to the station was a grand house with an impressive set of gates, of the sort that typically belonged to families who had owned the land for generations.

Buildings that had stood the test of time rubbed shoulders with newly built detached houses; flats with all kinds of modern conveniences found themselves alongside those whose wear and tear stood out for a mile. There were houses where celebrities lived and there were also, as Taro had discovered from the listings online, flats that didn't even have baths in them.

The people who constructed these buildings must have had some kind of mission they wished the buildings to fulfil, some form of hope for them, but looking at the area in general, it was hard to see any kind of communality or purpose at all. It seemed more like the place was the result of everyone's individual ideas and contingent circumstances commingling, all their little details then driving them further from one another over time. Somehow the thought put Taro's mind at ease. It made him feel better about the fact that, somewhere in the midst of all that, he spent entire days just lolling about on the floor and napping.

Taro began to get better at spotting empty houses. Just like Nishi had said, houses that were empty gave off a fundamentally different feeling than those with people living in them. Even vacant houses that were well looked after, so that it might appear at first as though they just had nobody at home, he came to be able to recognize quickly as actually uninhabited. There were so many different types of empty houses, flats and offices, too. The train he took to work ran along an elevated rail track, and from it he could see into the rooms on one floor of all the office buildings and blocks of flats that the train passed.

Taro found it peculiar that there should be so many homes without people living in them. Across the country, far away from here, there were areas losing the vitality they'd once had, and there were shopping arcades close to major stations that now lay deserted, their shutters permanently down. The shopping arcade close to the flat Taro had grown up in was the same, dark during the day. But that was vacant property in places where whole areas were in decline. Compared to those, the vacant houses in this city, which people were still flooding to from all across Japan and whose rent prices now beggared belief, didn't carry with them such desolation or gravity. Rather, they seemed more like hidden caverns he'd happened to stumble across. All around, enormous buildings and blocks of flats were being constructed day by day, and yet, hidden away on the inside, there were secret caves. It brought to mind the cracks that formed inside daikon radishes when you left them out for a while without eating them, although then Taro thought about how those vacant houses would be lived in again some day, and how buildings could be demolished and built again, so they weren't really so similar to daikon after all. He tried thinking of them instead in terms of sponges, or holey cheese, but couldn't quite seem to land on the right metaphor.

Taro wondered what would happen if someone were to sneak inside one of those vacant houses and begin living there. Would they be found out? For sure there would be no running water or gas or anything like that, but then he also had come across a few houses with signs alerting people they had well water they could provide to others in the case of an earthquake. As long as you had water, you could manage somehow. These were the places his thoughts carried him to, though he had no actual intention of testing these ideas out.

Behind the shopping arcade that led away from the station, to one side of a road he passed on the first of his three routes to work, was an uninhabited house with a reasonably sized garden. The smallish car parked inside the gates must have been there for years; there were weeds growing inside it. How did that happen? Had the bottom fallen out, or what? The evergreen trees in the garden had grown so high that they were wound around the utility pole, and their foliage was now dangling towards the houses on the other side of the street. From the gaps in the wooden fence in the front of the house, he could see the sunroom attached to the single-storey house. The sunroom had no storm shutters, only regular windows, and then, on the inside, latticed paper screens, which were shut. Some light was making its way through the paper of the screens, so the inside of the house wouldn't be pitch black. The tatami would be mouldy, and there would be a few bits of abandoned furniture, in the same way that the bike and laundry rack, now rusted, had also been left. Time inside the house was a cycle of murky days and nights of total darkness. You'd sometimes hear the sound of rats echoing through the ventilation shaft. For some reason Taro could imagine the scene inside the house vividly, could picture it in as much detail as rooms that he'd actually seen.

Then, one day, all that was left of it was an empty lot. In the place where it should have been, unchanged from the week before, there was now, quite abruptly, nothing. The overgrown trees, the single-storey house, the small car and the weeds were all gone, and Taro found he couldn't remember what else had been there to begin with.

There was another plot of razed land diagonally opposite from that house. Taro could not remember what had been there before either. In yet another plot, which had been vacant for as long as he could remember, construction work had now begun. He suddenly began paying attention to signs announcing demolition, or announcing who had commissioned forthcoming construction on the site.

He realized that next year or the year after, a similar sign would appear outside his own block of flats, and tried picturing it. There would be nobody moving into the empty flat next to his or the one next to that. He had peered through the window of the flat next to his, and at the back of the dim space, a closet with its fabric door was ripped and left wide open. Everything awaited demolition. Taro was suddenly visited by the thought that he better start thinking about where he was going to move to.

When he saw Nishi, she would greet him in a way that seemed friendly, but there was something a bit distant about the way she acted. She didn't drop by his flat, or start conversations. Perhaps, he thought, she was embarrassed about having drunk too much and spoken more than she meant to.

When Taro returned home from work in the evening, he could always see from the street that lights were on in the Dragon Flat, but he never caught sight of her on the balcony. Sometimes he saw Mrs Snake sticking her head over her balcony railing, seemingly looking in the direction of his flat.

Midway into June was supposed to be the time when the rainy season came. That year there wasn't a great deal of rain, but it was always overcast.

Every day, the sky was slathered with a layer of low, thick clouds. Taro's cloud daydream didn't get triggered on days when it was so cloudy that there was no sky in sight, or on rainy days either. At these times, he stopped being able to imagine that there was anything above the clouds at all. Beyond them, he imagined, was neither blue sky, nor dark cosmos, but just see-through space, stretching on and on with nothing to fill it.

The first time Taro had been in an aeroplane, it had been raining. The aeroplane had risen through the rain-clouds, their insides like dry-ice vapour, and then emerged above the clouds, into a bright blue sky. Taro was flabbergasted. He felt quite unnerved, thinking that he might have moved into a different world from the one he thought existed. But the tops of the bright white clouds that he peered down on from the double-paned windows, with their fierce brightness and their overpowering mass and scope, were just like the ones that had appeared in his visions. It seemed uncanny that he could have known about them, could have pictured them with such clarity, when he had never once seen them before. He kept scanning the tops of the clouds for people walking about, but couldn't spot anyone. Frost spread its way like snowflakes between the two panes of glass.

When the plane passed over gaps between the clouds, Taro saw the ocean and the land beneath. He saw coastlines with the same contours that he knew from maps. As his mind made these connections, he had a visceral realization that the world as it existed in his head and the ground that he walked on every day were actually the same place. From that time on, he had been a fan of aeroplanes.

Taro's father had died without having once boarded a plane. He had rarely been on holidays of any kind, except for his fishing trips. He would talk about America a lot, declaring that America was such and such, or saying that in a situation like this one, the US Government would do such and such, but he had never once left Japan, let alone visited the States.

Last New Year, his mother had gone to Hawaii for the third time, and he was pretty sure his sister had been to both New York and San Francisco, but Taro found all the preparation for going abroad such a hassle that the only time he'd been overseas was on his honeymoon to Italy. His clearest memory was the ruins of an old market he'd seen there.

When he had time to kill between coming home from work and going to bed, Taro would look through *Spring Garden*. He tried comparing the pictures in the book to the house that he could see from his balcony.

The fact that he shared a first name with the man who had taken some of those photos and who appeared in others, though, didn't give rise to any real interest on his part. Nishi had gone on about how much she liked the unpretentiousness of Kaiko Umamura's expression, and how the couple's intimacy seemed to radiate naturally from the photos, and how the feel of the house seemed to be connected to their relationship, but Taro wasn't struck by any of those things especially.

For sure, these were the sorts of natural expressions you'd expect to see in people's private photos, but when you looked at a whole book's worth of them, they came to seem a little *too* natural. The exquisiteness of all the aged furniture and the low table with exactly the right amount of clutter seemed to Taro *too* perfect to be trusted. That was especially true of Taro Gyushima—the expressive look on his face in each photo, his long, dishevelled hair arranged to look as if he hadn't laid a finger on it, his white shirt intended to seem like it was his everyday attire. Even the angle at which he turned seemed calculated to look casual. Taro didn't like men like that, who were always thinking about how they were coming across. It was maybe that feeling that prevented him from being able to simply enjoy looking at the photos.

Nevertheless, when he thought about how these rooms actually existed inside the walls of that sky-blue house over the wall, he could at least understand Nishi's desire to go and see it with her own eyes.

On one of the last pages of the book was a shot of Taro Gyushima in the garden. He was standing over to the right, in front of the plum and the pine, digging with a spade. He wore the same white shirt even when gardening, but in this shot alone he was paying more attention to what he was doing than to the camera, or at least, so it seemed to Taro. The hole was about one metre in diameter, and twenty or thirty centimetres deep. When Taro compared this to the other photos, the shrubbery around looked different, so he guessed that he might have been transplanting something.

When Taro was hanging his laundry out on the balcony, he looked in the direction of the house, but he couldn't see the garden. The trees and the ivy in Mrs Saeki's garden were growing wilder by the day, and the branches of the maple that overhung the wall were now poking their way into Taro's balcony. There were crows cawing at each other. It sounded as if they were having a conversation. Taro suddenly remembered Numazu's story about burying Cheetah in his garden. The hole Taro Gyushima was digging might have been to bury something, he thought. Maybe that bird from the cage. It wasn't as though the photographs were arranged in chronological order, so maybe the bird had died, and he was burying it. Then again, he thought, that hole was far too big for burying a bird in.

Taro felt an itch on his foot, and realized he'd got his first mosquito bite of the summer.

One rainy Saturday at the end of June, Taro stepped out of his flat. He didn't really want to go out in the rain, but he didn't have any food that didn't require cooking, and so he'd decided to go to the convenience store to pick up a ready meal. Standing by the bottom of the stairs to the first floor were Nishi and Mrs Snake, chatting and pointing up at the branches of the tree that grew beside the staircase.

Taro didn't know the name of the tree, but it had thin branches and luminous green leaves. At the beginning of the summer before last, when he had first seen the tiny white flowers hanging on it, he had been surprised that a tree could produce anything so delicate and pretty. He remembered that it had flowered this year too, not long ago. After that, some clusters had formed on the tips of the branches, but the clusters were a strange shape that didn't seem to fit with the flowers. He didn't remember having seen them until last year, either. It seemed that it was those clusters that Mrs Snake and Nishi were pointing to now.

"What are those things?" Taro asked.

"They're galls," Mrs Snake replied.

"What's that?"

"A kind of plant tumour. They're caused by parasitic lice that make the buds mutate and change shape, and then larvae grow inside them. They only form on Japanese snowbells like this one. The 'cat's paw' part comes from their shape."

"I thought they looked like bunches of mini bananas, actually," Taro said. "But now that you mention cats, they seem less like paws and more like the tails on *nekomata*. You know, the demon-cats, with nine tails."

"It's foxes that have nine tails," Nishi corrected him, looking for some reason very pleased with herself. "*Nekomata* only have two."

Mrs Snake looked up at Taro, once again with a child-like gaze, and said, "There aren't any foxes around here, but there are raccoon dogs. Did you know that? There's a mother and her cub living by the tracks of the Setagaya line. I wonder what on earth they find to eat around here! They look a lot like badgers, but they're definitely raccoon dogs."

"And I thought this was supposed to be the city," Taro said.

Mrs Snake's eyes were sparkling. Taro had seen her speaking to cats by the side of the road several times, and imagined that she was something of an animal lover. Nishi was standing behind her, nodding silently.

That evening, Taro was eating a dinner of grilled mackerel in his flat when Mrs Snake brought him three illustrated guides: one for plants, one for birds, and one for wild animals.

"I'm sure they'll come in handy," she said, pressing them on him.

On a sudden whim, Taro asked her what kind of people had lived in the sky-blue house before. Kaiko Umamura and Taro Gyushima were no longer there when she moved in, she said. That was seventeen years ago. An American couple lived there for ten years, and after that, a family with two sons in high school. Taro vaguely remembered seeing the couple with the two sons at some point, but he had no clear mental image of them.

Mrs Snake said she had known the American couple a little, too. The husband was in Japan for his job, which had something to do with aircraft. The wife was often out tending the garden, and Mrs Snake would sometimes come across her while she was working in the flower beds by the front door. The woman didn't speak much Japanese, but she was friendly, and would greet Mrs Snake with a pleasant "Konnichiwa!". Feeling obliged to return her kindness, Mrs Snake would talk for a while, managing to get across in stilted English the fact that she liked Neil Young, and had been born in the same year as he was. She had been invited over to their house three times for dinner, and they played Neil Young for her on the big stereo in the living room. By that point, the tatami had been replaced by laminate flooring, but the pine was still in the garden, and the kitchen hadn't yet been renovated. Nishi, who Mrs Snake had told this to the other day, had been incredibly envious, she said.

Taro felt surprised to think that his dad, too, must have been born in the same year as Neil Young, but when he thought about it he realized he hardly knew Neil Young's music. He looked away from the shining eyes of Mrs Snake, who was still stood outside his front door, and said, "My father always had this really stereotypical image of rock music, or any music produced by any kind of band, as being about young people in scruffy clothes making as much noise as possible. In fact, I got told off for buying a guitar. Of course, my father lived until he was eighteen in the mountains in Shikoku, so I guess his way of thinking was a bit behind compared with other people of his generation."

"Even where I grew up, they thought of me as a kind of rebel, and that was in the suburbs of Tokyo. I really do miss those times, you know. I went to see the Beatles when they came to Japan. I still feel proud about that."

"Wow, that's amazing."

"Is your father in good health?"

"Actually no, he passed away almost ten years ago."

"Really, I'm sorry to hear that. He must have been young."

As Mrs Snake spoke, her voice sounded choked up and her eyes grew moist. Taro looked at her curiously. Why would you cry about the death of someone you'd never met, the father of someone you weren't particularly close to?

Mrs Snake stayed for a while longer in Taro's doorway, reminiscing about the past. Taro learnt many things: She'd been born in a town called Tanashi, which had become a subdivision of Tokyo, and had been renamed. Until a few years ago, she had taught sewing at a fashion design college. She had been to see the Beatles playing the Budokan, and also travelled to America to see Neil Young. Neil Young was Canadian. When Mrs Saeki, now in a care home, had married into the Saeki family and had first come to live here, the land all the way over to the railway tracks had been fields, and the family had owned all of it (although Mrs Snake thought that might be a bit of an exaggeration). Mrs Saeki's husband, who had passed away, had been the headmaster of a junior high school, and before Taro had moved into the Pig Flat, there had been a Chinese girl, a student, living there.

At the end of June, Numazu, the colleague of Taro's who had married a woman from Kushiro and changed his name to hers, left the company and moved to Kutchan, in Hokkaido, to work in a hotel with his wife.

When Taro asked Numazu if he'd be living close to his wife's parents, Numazu chuckled, and said that Kutchan was 400 kilometres from Kushiro; it was a seven-hour drive, the same distance as between Tokyo and Osaka. Taro didn't feel particularly happy about being treated so condescendingly, given that until very recently Numazu hadn't known the first thing about Hokkaido. On Numazu's last day at work, Taro gave him the cuckoo clock that he'd received from Nishi and that had been stuffed in his closet all this time.

The weather was beginning to get hot and sticky, and Taro took to leaving the glass door to his balcony open, and just pulling the screen door shut. The mesh had started to fray, however, and the screen door itself would often come off the track. One day, while Taro was trying to fix a hole in the mesh, the screen door came off its track again. He was considering just leaving it to spare himself the annoyance when he noticed a round stone wedged in the right corner of the track. He crouched down to pick it up and found that, instead, it was a tiny, round vessel about one or two centimetres in size, about the same as the tip of his finger.

Taro got a torch, and tried shining it on the thing. It seemed to be some kind of miniature urn or vase, the upper section tapered, like the neck of a saké flask. It was grey in colour, and as evenly and exquisitely shaped as if it had been formed on a potter's wheel. It was as hard as cement. Taro had never seen anything like it before, and assumed that it was the egg sac of an insect, or else some kind of nest.

Feeling a little creeped out, Taro closed the glass door gently, then realized that where the tiny vase had been wedged, in one of the grooves in the track, was exactly the place where it would not be crushed by the door.

Taro regretted that there was no illustrated guide to insects among the books that Mrs Snake had given him.

He tried an internet search on his phone, entering terms like "vase", "insect" and "nest", and found several images that looked quite like the thing that he'd discovered. It seemed to be the nest of a "potter wasp". The wasp would lay an egg inside the vase, deposit the larvae of other insects as food for the wasp larva, then seal the vase. The wasp supposedly made a separate vase for each of its larva. Taro checked his balcony and window frames for other tiny vases that might be lying around, but he couldn't find any.

The article went on to explain that when the potter wasp larva emerged from its egg and developed into an adult, it would break open the lid of the vase and emerge. The vase that Taro had found was without a lid, which meant the wasp that had been born inside must have already flown its nest. Taro examined the tiny vase again. The inside was pitch black, and he couldn't see a thing. That tiny bit of darkness seemed bottomless to him.

Taro then tried doing a search for "cat's paw gall" and "Japanese snowbell". The site he found had plenty of details and many close-up photos of the galls, tightly packed with squirming insects. Overcome by disgust, Taro quickly closed the page.

With the tasks that he had to take over because of Numazu's departure, as well as the training of the new staff member assuming Numazu's role, Taro had a very busy summer. It was an especially hot summer, too, and every time he left the office to visit a client, the rays of the sun and the body heat of everyone crammed on the trains sapped his strength. On his way to work, he had to transfer at Shinjuku. Just when he'd been thinking that the engineering works that had been going on there forever had finally been completed, he noticed that new engineering works had now begun on a different set of tracks. When Taro had visited Tokyo for the first time thirteen years before, to attend a training course for the first hair salon he'd worked at, there had been engineering works ongoing then, and they had been going on ever since, in some part of the station or other. In the last few years, it had been large-scale engineering works that had affected the entire station.

Now the realization struck Taro: the works would never come to an end. They would finish only when the station had ceased to be used. Every day, Taro got home late at night and went straight to bed, turning the air conditioning on so he'd be able to sleep in that stuffy apartment, not bothering to open the windows. The air-conditioning unit had to be over ten years old. It certainly produced plenty of noise, but it didn't do much in the way of making the room comfortable. It was either so powerful that he would feel chilled, or it did nothing to cool the room at all. It was like it had sensed the fate awaiting it in a year or two, and had stopped caring about its job performance. The rumbling from the fridge, too, had become more frequent, and it sometimes woke Taro. It sounded like a motorbike engine revving up.

Mrs Snake would come over from time to time, bringing souvenirs purchased from places she'd been, or sharing presents that people had given her. When Taro received some cookies that a colleague had brought back from a holiday overseas, he took them over to Mrs Snake's flat, hoping to repay her kindnesses. It was the first time that he'd ever been up to the first floor.

From the doorway to Mrs Snake's flat, where he stood, he could see that she had very little furniture, and hardly any other stuff either. The only furniture he could see was a cabinet for dishes in the kitchen and a low table in the tatami room. Not even a TV. That kind of minimalist interior, which made her place look a lot more spacious than his flat did, was different from what he'd been expecting, based on Mrs Snake's clothes and her way of speaking. The fact that it was tidy came as no surprise, and neither did the purple flowers arranged meticulously in the vase on top of the shoe cabinet, nor the cushions laid out, nor the traditional Japanese fabric in navy and maroon, which seemed similar to the kind of clothes she wore. It was that the room went beyond mere tidiness to something spooky. Taro felt that things he would have expected to be there, things that should have been there, were missing. It lacked the feel of being lived in, a bit like a room at a ryokan, or a cheap motel.

The thought crossed his mind that it was already like an uninhabited place. Taro then hurriedly attempted to get rid of that thought. Mrs Snake invited him in for a cup of tea, but he declined. He returned to his own flat, where he began to regret his behaviour slightly.

He ran into Nishi on his way home from work, in the convenience store outside the station. As they walked back to their block of flats together, he mentioned how tidy Mrs Snake's flat was, and Nishi told him that she wanted to take a leaf out of Mrs Snake's book, that her own flat was so crammed full of stuff that there was barely space for her, even though it wasn't long before she'd have to move out.

Taro asked if Mrs Snake had always lived alone, and Nishi told him that she'd been married once, but that her ex-husband had come from a very strict, traditional family. Mrs Snake had moved in with the family, as was convention, but her mother-in-law had been very hard on her, and she had eventually been driven out, forced to leave her two-year-old son behind.

As they reached the front of the block of flats, Nishi mentioned that the bulb in her ceiling light needed changing, but that she was too short to manage it. She asked Taro if he'd mind helping her.

Just as Nishi had warned, the hall, the kitchen and the main tatami room were a cluttered mess. Every available bit of wall space was filled with shelves heaving with boxes and books, the gaps between crammed with trinkets and paper.

"It's times like these when I think about how handy it would be to have a man around. Like, when I'm trying to open a jar, or carrying heavy luggage. I get over it soon enough, mind you."

"You could have left that last bit out."

"You're right. That'll teach me for trying to be funny."

"Yeah, I gave that up a long time ago."

On a shelf, painted a similar shade of blue as the house, was a single-lens reflex camera. Taro was by no means an expert, but it looked vintage. The top of the camera was raised into a silver triangle, a bit like a pointed roof, and it struck Taro that the shape resembled the roof of the sky-blue house. The large lens had no cap, and the inside of its cylinder was dark. He thought of the darkness inside the potter wasp's nest. Both the camera itself and all the things around it were conspicuously dusty, and Taro imagined that Nishi probably hadn't touched the camera since putting it on the shelf.

On the table beside the balcony were a large computer monitor and a white panel-shaped device with a stylus. The space around them was buried in comics, books, pens and cups.

"Is this what people these days use to draw manga?"

"People draw their first drafts by hand. Usually with felt pen, sometimes with acrylic paint. Then you scan those drawings in and neaten up the fine details using a tablet."

"Do you have any books of your stuff?"

"Ha! I'm flattered, but please don't feel you need to show interest."

Actually, Taro hadn't been asking out of politeness, but simple curiosity. Still, whether Nishi was just shy or she actually didn't want him to see her stuff, she wouldn't even tell him her pen name.

He replaced the bulb, and began putting on his shoes to leave. Nishi promised that she would do something as a thank you next time, but Taro told her not to worry about it. When he walked into his flat, the fridge began its usual rumbling.

It finally started getting cooler around the end of September, and halfway through October, Taro's workload began to ease a little.

One sunny Sunday afternoon, Taro opened the door to his balcony. No sooner had he looked towards the sky-blue house than the stained-glass window with the two dragonflies opened upwards, and Nishi's face popped out of it. It was the window on the landing, where Taro Gyushima was posing with his twin-lens reflex camera in *Spring Garden*. Seeing Nishi's face in his line of sight caught Taro by surprise and he started, letting out a noise at almost exactly the same time as Nishi made one too. Yet Nishi didn't look very surprised. In fact, come to think of it, Taro had never seen Nishi looking particularly shocked, or angry, or overjoyed.

"You know trespassing is a serious crime, right?"

"Oh, no, it's nothing like that! I've become friends with Mrs Morio."

Nishi lowered her voice as she spoke, so Taro couldn't catch what she was saying.

Then he heard a child's voice calling her. It sounded like the boy.

Nishi turned around and answered "Coming!" then shut the window.

Taro stared up at the stained-glass window that was now back in place. He hadn't known that the window could be opened.

In the evening, Nishi rang at the door of Taro's flat, and the two of them headed out to the restaurant they'd been to in May. Taro ordered plates of deep-fried chicken and deep-fried octopus. Nishi drank a beer, and explained to Taro how she'd come to see the house.

It was in the middle of September, when it was still very hot and humid. After sundown Nishi had set out on her daily circle of the block, and was passing in front of the Morios' house when she saw something lump-like lying in the street. She thought it might be a cat, but then realized it was too big for a cat. Then the lump got up and walked on two legs. Nishi saw a car passing through the intersection ahead and decided the situation was dangerous. She went up and spoke to the child. The child turned around, and said, "Where's Mummy?"

Nishi saw that it was the little Morio girl. She took the girl by the hand and led her over to the house, where she pressed the intercom buzzer, but there was no reply. She pressed it again, and this time heard a frantic-sounding voice calling out, "Just a moment!" The door was flung open and the child's mother came out.

"Excuse me, I think I found your child."

At the same time as Nishi said this, the woman cried out, "Yuna!" and the little girl instantly began sobbing.

"I found her in the street. She was just standing there..." Nishi offered in explanation, but the mother was clasping her child tightly to her, comforting her, and it seemed as though Nishi's words fell on deaf ears. She did afterwards thank Nishi, bowing over and over again so that Nishi bowed in return, and then the mother and child disappeared inside the house.

When she passed in front of the Morios' house at ten o'clock the next morning, Mrs Morio was out on the first-floor balcony, hanging out her laundry. She called out to Nishi, and asked her to wait. In a short time, she appeared at the front door, and apologized to Nishi for her rudeness the previous night. She had been in such a panic, she said, she had barely even said thank you. Nishi said, "Not at all," then explained that she lived in the block of flats behind the house and had just happened to be passing by at that time. Mrs Morio thanked her several more times, then invited Nishi in for a cup of tea.

"Are you sure?" Nishi asked, staring into the woman's face. She looked considerably younger than Nishi herself, and had an open, friendly smile.

"Of course! Come on in."

Mrs Morio gestured inside the house behind her with her right hand. Nishi entered through the bramble-entwined metal gates and went up the three porch steps to the house.

Seeing the stained glass with its pattern of irises up close for the first time, Nishi noticed how the thick glass diffused the light, dyeing the air in the front hall into a tissue of different colours in a way she found very beautiful.

After taking off her shoes in the entranceway, easily large enough for someone to sleep in, Nishi stepped into the hall with its hardwood floor. When Mrs Morio opened the door on the left, the influx of light was so blinding that Nishi nearly reeled. The living room she was shown into was even larger than she'd expected. The sunlight streaming into the room from the south bounced off the polished floor.

Covered in natural cotton, the corner sofa that looked out over the garden was as big as a bed. Without any sense of agency, like in dreams where her body stopped moving, Nishi sank into its softness. She felt almost as though she was floating. There was a vase of small white flowers on the oval low table right in front of her.

Mrs Morio brought over two cups of *hojicha* and some oatmeal cookies that she said she'd made.

Her name was Miwako. Her son was Haruki, and her daughter Yuna. Haruki, who was about to turn five, was suffering from bad asthma attacks, and Miwako had barely slept in days. Yesterday, she said, she'd nodded off beside his bed, and that was when her three-year-old daughter had slipped outside.

"I had no idea she was tall enough to reach the door handle," she said, sincere in her concern and astonishment. She was pale-skinned, not overweight but nicely rounded. Her way of speaking gave the impression of an incredibly earnest person, the kind who made everyone around her feel secure. On that visit, Yuna was at nursery, but Haruki was in bed upstairs. Nishi told Miwako that she'd had bad asthma as a child too, and it had always acted up at this time of year when the seasons were changing, so she understood her worry fully. At this, Miwako opened her eyes wide and leant forward, saying that she herself had been such a healthy child she'd rarely caught a cold, and had never known anyone with asthma. As a result, she felt terribly anxious that she couldn't properly understand the suffering her son was going through and that she wasn't dealing with it in the right way.

"The fact that he has to go through something like this when he's so young..." she said, and her eyes welled up with tears. Nishi listened to what Miwako had to say, then talked about her own symptoms and experiences in the hope that it might be of some use. When she explained that asthma often went away as children got older, and that she'd stopped having attacks by the time she started high school, Miwako nodded firmly and said, "I know it's important that I stay strong through all of this. It's him that's suffering, after all, not me."

Just then they heard a call of "Mummy", and the boy came down the stairs. He was in his pyjamas, but didn't look too poorly at all. Maybe his asthma wasn't as bad in the daytime, Nishi thought. Prompted by his mother, Haruki said hello to Nishi, and bowed politely.

Nishi asked him a couple of questions, but she had almost no experience of interacting with kids and wasn't quite sure how to go about it. Instead, she reached for a nearby sketchpad, and started drawing a selection of animals and cartoon characters, which the boy seemed delighted by. When Nishi explained that illustrating was her job, Miwako looked at her with eyes sparkling and said, "I'm so envious of people with talent!"

Miwako was from Hokkaido, she told Nishi. While at university in Sapporo, she had taken a part-time job in a hotel restaurant, and it was there that she had met Mr Morio, who had come to stay in the hotel on business. She had got married immediately after graduating, and moved to Tokyo. For that reason, she had no friends nearby, and tended to stay in the house by herself. She invited Nishi to come and see her again.

Miwako seemed to Nishi like the sort of person who would have no difficulty making friends, but she said that the other mothers at the private nursery her kids went to thought about nothing except how their children could be given the best possible education. They were very group-oriented, she said, and always on top of the latest information about learning, which made Miwako draw back. Something about the phrase "always on top of the latest information" brought a smile to Nishi's face, and Miwako said, "Sorry, I don't know why I used that expression," and smiled in embarrassment.

They had moved into the house because her husband had taken a fancy to it, she said, but he was so busy heading up a new project at his company that he often had to work on weekends as well, and there were few people in the neighbourhood of a similar age to her. All these things that Miwako had been storing up inside her came pouring out now to Nishi.

"Gosh, yes, it must be really hard for you. It is a pretty elderly neighbourhood around here, isn't it?"

As Nishi spoke, she looked around the room at the bright white walls and laminate flooring—different from how it was in *Spring Garden*.

She thought about how, twenty years ago, this room had been a Japanese-style room complete with tatami and that antique dresser. Now, there was a low television stand with a fifty-inch screen perched on top of it. The ornamental panels with the elephants were still there above the doors, but the wicker chairs in the sunroom were gone, replaced by a couple of round green padded armchairs. The grass in the garden had a slightly bleached look. Nishi could see the crepe myrtle to the left, and the crabapple next, and the plum to the right. There was no sign of the pine or the stone lantern that had been part of that garden twenty years before.

There was a child's drawing hanging in a white frame on one of the white walls. The lines traced in red crayon could have been either a flower or a fish. On the display shelf below it was a row of photographs: the Morios' wedding day, and the children when they were younger. There had been a photo framed in Kaiko Umamura's illustrations too, Nishi remembered. She had the feeling it had been a photo of a goldfish.

Miwako, noticing Nishi's roaming gaze, smiled a little embarrassedly, and said that she knew that it was a privileged sort of concern to have, but she found the house so big and fancy that often, when it was just herself and her kids here, it made her feel uneasy. She'd always wanted to live somewhere closer to nature, where she'd have a sense of the seasons passing. Before moving into this house, she said, they'd lived in a flat in Meguro, in the heart of Tokyo, but despite the years she'd lived there she'd never got used to how many buildings there were, and how little green. She also told Nishi that although the garden was small, it was her favourite thing about the house.

"It's a great garden," Nishi said. Through the window, she looked at the birds in the trees, flitting between their branches.

When Miwako had first come to Tokyo and found herself with more time than she knew what to do with, she had spent it all making cakes and biscuits, but now, she said, if she found herself with spare time again, she'd like to get a few planters and grow some vegetables. Then she looked at the clock on the wall and hurriedly stood up, apologizing for having kept Nishi so long.

Nishi would have visited the Morios' house every day if she could, but she didn't want to be thought of as pushy or annoying, so she decided to limit her visits to once or twice a week around lunchtime, or in the evening after the nursery bus had brought the children home, staying for no more than a couple of hours each time.

Playing with the kids allowed Nishi to explore many different parts of the house. The stair railing, patterned with brambles similar to those fabricated on the front gates, was just as it appeared in the photo book. She learnt that the stained-glass window on the landing could be opened. The sash windows were in a room with parquet flooring, which was used as the children's room. The room facing the balcony was still floored with tatami as in the pictures from twenty years ago, though now it had a large reclining sofa in it.

In general, more of the interior had stayed the same than Nishi was expecting, but all of it was now the Morios' house. It was the house in the photo book, but it was also, now, the house belonging to the Morios. She couldn't decide if the feeling of those two different houses coinciding perfectly in some places and varying in others was uncomfortable or interesting, and with the question still unresolved in her mind, she went around looking for the little details Kaiko Umamura had depicted in her illustrations, lounging around in the same spaces that appeared in the photo book. At the very least, when she was looking from the living-room sofa through the sunroom out at the garden, Nishi felt totally content. The rays of the setting sun would shine right where she was sitting, and she could hear almost no sounds at all except for the calls of the birds outside. The floor of the sunroom had been worn down and was becoming whitish in places. It seemed as though the decades that had passed there before and the afternoon now slipping by were coming together as one.

What Mrs Morio had said about her husband not being around much definitely seemed to be true, and about a month had passed before Nishi got to meet him when he came home from work.

When the two were introduced, he kept his hands neatly by his side and bowed politely to Nishi, saying, "Thank you ever so much for keeping my wife company."

It turned out he was the same age as Nishi.

The previous week, Nishi had gone with Miwako and Haruki, still off sick, to a nearby park. Nishi remarked to Haruki, who was worried about being away from nursery for so long, that she knew the evenings were really hard for him but in the day he was full of beans, wasn't he, and as he nodded his agreement, Haruki finally let his face relax into a smile.

The park wasn't so big, but it had a playing field about the size of a basketball court, surrounded by wire fencing. There, Nishi and Haruki played a slow game of catch with a rubber ball. Haruki was good at catch, as it turned out, and even as Nishi gradually extended the distance between them, he continued to throw the ball in a straight line towards her. Miwako, who said she was no good at ball sports, stood watching, letting out cries of admiration for both Haruki's and Nishi's throws.

From the age of four through to the age of ten, Nishi had been given intensive baseball training by her dad. Every day, from six in the morning, and then from five thirty in the afternoon after her dad had finished work at the factory, they would practice pitching and fielding in the park on the estate. Her father wanted to do something to build up the physical strength of his asthmatic daughter, and he was convinced that, since the times were changing and women in the future would have more freedom to do what they wanted, it was better to do things differently from other people. It also seemed as though he was trying, through her, to reclaim his own childhood, a childhood he had missed because his family had been too poor for him to enter any sports club at school. He told Nishi about his dream of producing Japan's first female professional baseball player, just like Yuki, the heroine of a Shinji Mizushima manga that he had read over and over. Nishi watched reruns of the cartoon series based on that manga, and really felt like the gutsy Yuki was the image of herself in the future. She believed that, just like Yuki, she would fight and win, and so, apart from the times when her asthma was really bad, she practised every day. Her father had no experience of playing baseball himself, so he read books written by famous players and coaches, and put together a practice schedule for her accordingly.

After Nishi started primary school, on weekends she visited the batting centre close to the factory where her dad worked. At those times her brother, who was one year younger than her, would tag along, but her father said that male professional baseball players were ten a penny, and that besides, boys should grow up to be brave and strong, and choose their own path, even if it meant breaking the rules a little. After watching a bunch of Jackie Chan movies, her brother took up karate, but packed it in after a few months. It was the summer of Nishi's fourth year in school when her father decided that she didn't have what it took to be a professional baseball player. By that time Nishi, who had always turned down requests from friends to play after school or on the weekend, no longer got invited by other kids to do things. When she was left alone in the classroom at break and after school while all the others were in their various clubs, she read the Osamu Tezuka manga series *Phoenix* and drew pictures in the margins of her notebook or the back of flyers. In other words, Nishi said, it had been her early spell of baseball that had led to her developing the talents to do her current job, which she liked, and that was one of the reasons she believed that she had luck on her side. In the fifth year, a girl who entered the class from another school was given the seat next to Nishi, and soon enough, the two began chatting to one another. Through her friendship with that new girl, Nishi began to be included by the other kids too.

The last time her years of baseball training had proved useful was when she'd started her first job. She and fourteen colleagues had been out drinking, and decided to go to a batting centre. In a game called Strike Out!—where you had to bat the ball and hit nine panels in a grid—Nishi had knocked down seven panels, coming in first among her colleagues, thoroughly surprising them. Being drunk, Nishi had really wanted to tell her father right then and there how happy she was for his training, but her parents had divorced before she'd gone to senior high school and she no longer had any way of contacting him.

Haruki, who was in top spirits after having his ball skills complimented by Nishi, announced with a gleam in his eye that he wanted to be a baseball player when he grew up. When Nishi saw him again not long after, he'd decided he wanted to play either for the New York Yankees or the Texas Rangers, at which point Nishi realized how much more international baseball had become since she was a kid, when it had all been about Japanese teams.

Yuna, his sister, was at the age where she was picking up new words at great speed, and would ask Nishi all kinds of questions. Nishi had never been good at interacting with children, but she found that listening to the slightly bizarre things that Yuna came out with was fun. Miwako said her husband had told her he was relieved to see her looking more cheerful.

"Is that really true?" Taro asked as he squeezed a wedge of lemon over their second plate of deep-fried chicken. "You didn't just lie your way in there?"

"Honestly, I can hardly believe it myself that an opportunity like this landed in my lap the way it did. Mrs Morio is just such a good-hearted person. The kind of person who doesn't understand what it even means to distrust someone, you know? I sometimes wonder if it's safe, you know, inviting people loitering outside your house inside, but people like her attract positive energy, I think. I get the feeling that family will be blessed somehow, whatever happens. It's weird to think that those amazing families you sometimes read about in magazines actually exist, though, isn't it? It's kind of incredible."

Nishi was on her sixth beer.

"If that's true, then why did you have to keep it from me?"

"I didn't want to jinx it. It's a rule of mine not to broadcast things until they've happened. I didn't tell anyone the university I was applying to until I got in, and I didn't tell my friends I was drawing comics, either, until I made it."

Nishi ordered beer number seven.

"It has happened, though, already. Isn't this exactly what you wanted?"

"But I still haven't managed to see the bathroom. To get to it, you have to go through a big washroom with sinks and stuff, so you can't see it from the hall. That's my one wish, to see those lime-green tiles. If I can, I want to take a photo, from the same angle as that photo on the last page of the photo book."

As she spoke, Nishi chewed on an *umeboshi* from the dish of simmered sardines she had just ordered. Looking at her, Taro began to feel concerned. Nishi was the type of person who wouldn't have hesitation about exploiting a moment when Mrs Morio was distracted to sneak into the bathroom. Or else she might come up with some ruse in order to get in, like saying that her own bath was broken.

"You told Mrs Morio about the photo book, right?"

"Actually, no."

"What? You've kept that quiet?"

"Just think about it. If someone told you they'd been watching your house for ages, wouldn't you get a bit scared?"

"You wouldn't have to mention that part, though. You could just tell her about the book."

"Yeah, I guess."

Nishi tilted her head to one side and smiled. There was something affected about the gesture, and it irritated Taro a little. It made him think that for all her friendliness, Nishi was actually just using Mrs Morio.

"Don't you think it's time to call it a day? You've made it inside the house, and seen the garden."

"You're right, of course. I know that. But the thing is, there's no guarantee how long that house is going to be around for. It's fifty years old now. The housing market is good at the minute, and there are construction sites springing up all over. That one by the railway tracks, for example. That's going to be a fancy new apartment block."

Hearing this, Taro realized that the increase in new detached houses in the neighbourhood and all the renovation taking place was exactly what they were talking about on the news programmes, where they attributed it to the economy and the rush to purchase and fix things before the rise in consumption tax, and so on. He heard people speaking about the housing market when he visited clients, but he'd always thought it was something that bore no relation to his life. But on his way to the station, he saw building after building rigged with scaffolding and covered in plastic sheeting. Now the block of flats across the street from View Palace Saeki III was getting knocked down.

When her seventh beer was brought over, Nishi drained the first half in a single gulp, then said, "Everything in Tokyo happens so fast, doesn't it? There are these buildings going up and new shops opening all the time, and every time you speak to someone they tell you what the latest big thing is, or what's going to be the next one. Don't you think? It's like, things get better so quickly but then they deteriorate just as fast."

"Well, yeah, but Tokyo is a big city. I don't know if you can make that kind of sweeping generalization. The place where I first lived here was a pretty rundown area with a much more local feel to it, and there were quite a few housing estates and factories there."

"That's true. But when you live in this central part, you kind of forget about other parts of Tokyo, I think. It's like you almost forget that other places apart from this one even exist. I've think I've even forgotten the place I grew up in."

"I quite like it here, you know."

"In what way? What do you like about it?" Nishi folded her arms and placed them on the table, then stared straight at Taro.

"I guess I like the fact there's just so much going on. That cat's paw thing on the tree, for example."

"That's Tokyo for you?"

"Well, this is the first place I've ever seen something like that."

"Isn't that because you haven't lived in many other places though?"

"Well, I guess, but..."

"Sorry, it's not like I can talk, either. Don't be offended, please."

"No problem."

All of the other customers had left the restaurant. The staff were looking at Nishi and Taro from behind the counter as if they wanted to start closing up. It seemed that closing time was earlier on Sunday.

"I'd love to have free rein of that house, just for a day," Nishi said with a sigh, and downed the last of her beer. When they left the restaurant, Nishi announced she was going to visit her mother in Chiba, and made towards the station.

From that day on, Nishi would sometimes bring round cookies, or pound cake, or biscuits that Miwako had made.

Taro always thanked her and accepted them, but since the time back in high school when he'd got food poisoning that had lasted for several days from an undercooked cheesecake his sister had made, he'd had an aversion to cookies or cakes that weren't shop-bought, so he took all of Miwako's handiwork into the office and gave it to his colleagues. They loved them, saying that the person who'd made them was clearly an expert at it, and that the kids who got to eat these kinds of things every day didn't know their luck. One colleague said how much he'd like to try pancakes this person had made. Then he gave Taro a list of the ten best places for pancakes in Tokyo, together with maps showing how to get to them.

One Sunday, at the end of October, Taro was lying on the tatami reading the news on his phone when he came across an article about an unexploded bomb.

On the morning of 27th October, approximately 1,150 people were temporarily evacuated from a residential district in the south of Shinagawa Ward in Tokyo while the Self-Defence Forces conducted a controlled explosion of an unexploded bomb belonging to the old Imperial Army. The bomb was discovered at a construction site in a residential area approximately 500 metres north of Ōimachi JR station. The municipal government dictated that all places in a 130-metre radius of the site should be cleared, and access prohibited. There was no disruption experienced to public transport. The Unexploded Ordnance Disposal Unit of the Eastern Army Combat Service Support Section created a protective wall around the site with large sandbags, and remotely detonated the device at just after 11 a.m. The evacuation order was repealed just after 1 p.m. According to a statement from the municipal authorities, the bomb was 15 cm in diameter and 55 cm in length.

The whole business seemed odd to Taro. He found it easy enough to imagine the bomb lying there underground, but the idea that a rusty old thing like that presented enough danger, after decades of being buried, to warrant such large-scale precautions and such a dramatic disposal struck him less as terrifying, and more like a simple error.

The bomb was probably the same age as his father, and Mrs Snake too. Maybe it had been made around the time they were born, and it had spent all those years, enough for someone to live a whole life, underground.

The following Monday was the anniversary of his father's death. Taro forgot about it, and remembered a few days after. Yet even when he remembered, there was nothing much to be done—after all, it had already come and gone. Then it occurred to him that, if nothing else, he could at least offer his father a beer. He took the mortar and pestle out of the cabinet, placed it in front of the TV, then placed a can of beer beside it. He wondered if he should put some flowers there as well. Strictly speaking, he was probably supposed to burn incense too, but he had neither flowers nor incense in his flat. In fact, neither of those items had entered his flat in the three years he'd been living there.

Even now, Taro sometimes had the feeling that his father wasn't dead, but had just gone out. The sensation was a bit like having a dream and forgetting the story halfway through. If his father had just gone out, though, he'd been gone for a really long time. He wondered if he had those kinds of thoughts because, in some way, he didn't want to accept his father's death. The same thing could probably be said of the fact he rarely went back to Osaka.

The leaves on the maple in Mrs Saeki's garden were turning orange and beginning to fall. The ivy was changing colour too, becoming such a bright red that it looked as though it was lit up from the inside.

Taro still walked to the station on the way to work, taking whichever of the three routes appealed to him on that particular day. The number of construction sites around seemed only to increase. He also came across places where they were tearing down buildings. He caught sight of what was left of a wooden house, loaded onto the back of a truck.

Every day, he walked over culverts with rivers running inside them. There were water pipes and gas pipes underground too, and maybe unexploded bombs, for all he knew. Back when he'd been working at the hair salon, he'd heard from an elderly customer that there had been bombs dropped during the war in the area closer to Shinjuku. If there were unexploded bombs still underground, then there must also be bits of the houses that were burnt down then, items of their furniture. Before that, this area had been fields and woods, and the leaves and fruits and berries that fell every year, as well as all the little animals, would also have formed layers over time, sinking down ever deeper under the ground.

And now Taro was walking on top of it all.

One night, when the breeze had started to get chilly, Taro came home straight from a client visit without calling back at his office, and got off at a different station from his usual. He'd set out walking in the direction of home when he saw an animal waddling across the tracks of the Setagaya line. At first, he took it for a fat, ungainly cat, but as he continued watching it, he realized it was a raccoon dog.

Skinny legs poked out from beneath its rounded body. Not pausing once, it kept on going, eventually disappearing into the bushes at the side of the tracks. Taro stood by the metal railing for a while, thinking about the unfamiliar shape of the animal he had just seen, trying to imprint it in his mind.

Around the middle of December, the couple in the Monkey Flat moved out. Taro had never exchanged a single word with them.

That left only three flats in View Palace Saeki III that were still lived in. With two people moving out at once—and the two who had made a lot of noise at that—Taro felt a sense of absence. The block was gradually edging closer to being uninhabited.

Taro spent New Year in the Pig Flat. From New Year's Eve through the second of January, there was no one else in the block. Taro kept his television on the entire time.

After the New Year's holiday was over, Taro noticed that the nameplate outside the concrete vault next door had vanished. There had never been any sounds from inside the house, so apart from the disappearance of the name-plate, the fact that the residents had moved out altered nothing. Taro asked Nishi about it when he ran into her outside the block one day, and she said that they'd left over a month ago. Nishi hadn't seen the move herself, though. Looking out at the house from his balcony, Taro saw that a plant abandoned on the roof had dried up and died, and it was then that he understood that there really had been people living in that house until relatively recently.

All the leaves had fallen from the snowbell, but the cat's paw gall still held on, though by now its little bunches had shrivelled up and turned black. The lice would have left a long time ago, which meant those nests, too, would be empty. Only the empty houses remained. The potter wasp's nest he'd discovered by his sliding door was still there, as he'd found it. Sometimes he went out and checked it, but no wasps went anywhere near it. Both the cat's paw galls and the vases were, he guessed, things that were used once and then never again. They were like houses that were destined to have one set of residents. There would be no new people coming to live in View Palace Saeki III either, though it was possible that new people would move into the concrete vault.

On his phone, Taro searched again for the page with the explanation of the cat's paw gall that he had previously closed in disgust. The pictures of insects were as gross as ever, but this time he tried to avert his eyes from the photos and focus on the text.

The louse that creates the cat's paw gall comes and goes between the Japanese snowbell and plants in the grass family, the article said, *repeatedly multiplying asexually and sexually. They can therefore only survive in regions that contain both kinds of plants.*

For a time when he was in high school, Taro used to think that evolution involved an element of will on the part of the creatures involved, so that to a certain extent, the form that living creatures took reflected their desire to become a particular way. He knew that, according to biology and evolutionary theory, that hypothesis of his wasn't correct, and now, when Taro learnt about the habitats of strange creatures like these, he thought, like everyone else, that they had been formed that way as the result of a process he didn't understand, and once they had turned out that way, they kept on going, repeating the same actions, endlessly. He could now accept that was all there was to it.

The only option available was to go on doing the same things endlessly, wondering why everything had to be such a pain, about how good it would be if you could eat leaves or fruit from some other kind of tree instead of the one you'd landed on. Once you could no longer go on repeating those actions, then you and your species, at least in its current form, would disappear.

The potter wasp's case seemed a bit simpler, but even with that, he thought what a pain it must be to make a different little vase for each new larva. Did having individual nests like that increase the chance of survival over having a big nest where all the young ones incubated together? Could living creatures be relied on to find the best solutions to their problems?

There was no way that Taro could even begin to answer such questions, but he felt like having one of those miniature vases to himself would be better than living packed tightly alongside all his brothers and sisters inside one of those cat's paw sacs.

One Saturday, the start of a three-day weekend, a delivery truck brought Taro two styrofoam boxes. They were from Numazu, sent from his new place in Kutchan. Taro had received an email from Numazu the previous evening, the first in ages. He said he'd finally settled into both his new home and his new job, and that he would be sending Taro some local specialities from Kushiro, so to keep an eye out for the delivery. He apologized that it had taken so long to thank Taro for the present of the cuckoo clock. It was the exact same clock his wife had seen in a shop and regretted not buying. She had been searching for one like it ever since, so she'd been overjoyed by the gift. It was even colder than he'd been expecting, he said, but it wasn't so bad. He'd attached a picture with his wife holding the clock. It was the first time Taro had seen a photo of Numazu's wife, and his first thought was that she looked like Numazu. Noting the unusual surname written in Numazu's handwriting in the SENDER box on the delivery form, he got the feeling that Numazu was now totally used to his new name.

Inside one box were three horsehair crabs. The other contained dried Atka mackerel and a jar of salmon roe. Taro regretted not telling Numazu that he didn't like dried fish. If he had done that, Numazu might have sent him something else, something he'd have liked. More salmon roe, or maybe some kind of squid, or fish cakes. In any case, there was far too much here for him, or anybody, to eat on his own.

Numazu knew that Taro lived alone, but he must have been trying to express the depth of his gratitude with these gifts. Taro had no idea about how to cook horsehair crabs, so he went up to the first floor and knocked on the door of the Snake Flat. There was no reply. He couldn't see any lights on inside, either, so he guessed Mrs Snake must be out. Come to think of it, he hadn't seen her around for a while. He felt sure she couldn't have moved out without saying anything, but it was possible that she was getting ready to move elsewhere. Taro then tried the Dragon Flat next door. As he knocked, it occurred to him that he'd received the cuckoo clock from Nishi in the first place, so the gift he'd received in return should by rights belong to Nishi too. She answered the door wearing a padded wide-sleeved kimono over a hooded sweatshirt and a thick woollen hat, yet her feet were bare.

When Taro told her about the seafood, Nishi suggested, eyes twinkling, that they take it over to the Morios' house.

Taro went back to his flat, ahead of Nishi. Alone, he found himself staring at the crabs. He'd never eaten horsehair crabs before. He studied the spines scattered across their shells, picking them up and turning them over, freaking out at their eyes sticking out from their shells, and so round and black that they didn't seem like real eyes at all. He was still doing this when Nishi came to the door. She'd changed out of her sweatshirt into a blue cardigan and grey trousers in a thick material, and looked smart. The Morios, she told him, didn't have dinner plans, so it was fine to go over. Mrs Morio had said that if there was salmon roe, then she'd prepare hand-rolled sushi. Nishi and Taro should definitely come over, she'd said, and they could eat all together.

Nishi knelt down beside the styrofoam boxes in Taro's kitchen, and began prodding the crabs.

"Time is running out for me," she said suddenly, as if she was delivering a dramatic line from a soap, then stood up and looked at Taro. "I'm moving out next month."

It turned out that Nishi's mother, who lived alone in a new town in the north part of Chiba, had been diagnosed with breast cancer four years ago. The tumour had been removed, and the cancer hadn't come back, but for six months she'd been prone to illness, so Nishi had decided to move in with her. Of late she'd been visiting once a week to help out, but it was really too far to commute. Her younger brother in Nagoya had newborn twins and was unable to get over to Tokyo easily. She had a reasonable amount of steady work now, had just got another contract for a weekly illustration slot on a website, so moving wasn't going to affect her career. Her mother's place was a flat in yet another housing estate, but it was on the sixth floor and surrounded by beautifully shaped zelkova trees, and the view from the window, at least, was great.

"So the thing is, I was wondering if I could ask you a favour."

Thinking he'd heard a very similar line from Nishi before, Taro resisted nodding.

"When we're at the Morios' and everyone's busy eating the crabs, I'm going to put a beer glass on the corner of the table. Could you please knock it over," Nishi said, gesturing to illustrate what she meant.

"You put a glass on the table, and I knock it over?" repeated Taro.

"Yes, because that way it'll go on my clothes, right? Then I'll say, 'Oh, do you mind if I use the bathroom to wash it off?'"

"The bathroom," Taro repeated.

"I'll make sure I get a tall glass, one that'll be easy to knock over."

"Right, yeah." Taro was making sure to be non-committal. One part of him felt Nishi should see this plan through on her own, but he was also curious to get a look inside the Morios' house himself. It was less that he wanted to make sure that it really was the same house in the photo book, and more that he wanted to see with his own eyes the sort of house that could bring about such fixation on Nishi's behalf.

At five o'clock, Nishi and Taro went over to the Morios' house, each carrying a styrofoam box of seafood. When they pressed the buzzer to the intercom by the gate, they heard a pattering sound and then the front door was wrenched open forcefully.

"Hello!" said the little boy and girl in unison. Miwako appeared behind them, and introduced herself to Taro, thanking him, telling him that crab was a big favourite of her kids, and saying she'd heard a lot about him from Nishi.

The children stood on either side of Nishi, each taking one of her hands, seeming as attached to her as the tales he'd heard.

Taro was shown into the large living room, which was filled with warm light. It made a pretty different impression from the photos in *Spring Garden*, Taro felt. Thinking about it, he realized that the book didn't contain a single shot taken after dark.

"Actually, I was hoping to see you soon anyway," Miwako said, looking at Nishi as she placed tea things on the low table. "We're having to move to Fukuoka. It's such bad timing. Just when I've finally found a friend in Tokyo."

In a slow, gentle tone, Mrs Morio recounted how her husband originally came from Fukuoka, where his parents ran a scientific materials company. The company he was currently working for was an affiliated firm, and he had always been destined to take over the whole business eventually, but his stepfather had fallen ill and so the change was happening sooner than expected. They were going to live in his parents' house, but would have one part of it all to them themselves—a part originally converted for Mr Morio's stepbrother and his family, who had since moved abroad for work. The house was a little way from the centre of the city, and close to the sea, which Mrs Morio thought might do Haruki's health good.

Nishi listened mostly without altering her expression, occasionally saying things to Yuna, who came padding over with her toys.

"My grandpa's house is huge. They've got a teddy bear that's this big. It looks exactly like a bear in a zoo!" Haruki exclaimed.

Looking at Haruki, stretching his arms wide and speaking with animation, Taro noticed that the boy's fringe was so long it was practically falling in his eyes.

"His hair's quite long, isn't it?" he said.

"You're right," Mrs Morio said. "It's too long. We've been so busy with this and that that I haven't had time to have it cut. I wish I could just do it myself but I made a mess of it once and ever since then he won't let me near it."

"Yeah, cos everyone in my class laughed at me!"

"I used to be a hairdresser, back in the day. I'll cut it for him, if you like."

Taro almost smiled at his own phrase, "back in the day". It was only three or four years ago he'd been a hairdresser, but there was no doubting the fact that, to him, it already felt like the distant past.

They sat Haruki on one of the chairs in the sunroom, spread out newspapers and bin bags around him, and then Taro began to cut the boy's hair with a pair of scissors that Miwako had. It had been a while since he'd held a pair of scissors, although these scissors designed for home use felt totally different from the sharpened professional ones he'd used at work. Still, their familiar snip seemed to resonate somewhere deep inside him. Taro still had two pairs of haircutting scissors put away in his closet. He hadn't decided how he felt about the whole hair-salon business. He hadn't made up his mind to give it up forever, but neither was he sure that he wanted to go back to it. It was a decision that he was avoiding making.

Through the windows of the sunroom Taro could make out the garden, illuminated by the lights from the house. The glass reflected the interior of the room, making it hard to get a good look out, but he could see enough to know that it was definitely the same one as in *Spring Garden*.

Taro looked over to the right corner of the garden, in front of the plum tree. It was too dark to say for sure, but it didn't seem like there was anything there. It was the place where Taro Gyushima in the photo book had been digging—either transplanting or burying something.

As Taro was cutting Haruki's fringe, he noticed that the boy kept sticking his fingers in his mouth. "What've you got in there?" he asked.

"Keigo's and Yuki's have come out already," Haruki said. With his tiny index finger, he was checking his bottom front teeth to see if they were wobbly.

From behind the kitchen counter, Miwako called out, "All his best friends' teeth are coming out, and he won't stop talking about it. I think he's scared of being the last."

Haruki opened his mouth wide to show Taro two neat little rows of blue-white teeth.

"If the baby teeth don't fall out soon, your adult teeth will start growing out of other parts of your body. Did you know that? Your hands and things."

Haruki looked petrified by this idea, so Taro immediately assured him he was kidding.

Taro thought about how he had believed until he was in high school that adult teeth fell out as easily as milk teeth did. He remembered asking one of his relatives, who was talking about the traumatic experience of having wisdom teeth removed, what was so bad about it, and having his question laughed at. All of Taro's wisdom teeth had grown in dead straight and he hadn't had to have a single one removed. He didn't know if he had his bone structure to thank for that, or what. People rarely told him that he looked like his father, but it seemed that they were alike in having good bones, at least.

The haircut was over in no time, and for a while Taro played with the two children. He'd spent a fair bit of time with his ex-wife's niece and nephew, so he was more used to dealing with kids than Nishi was. Hearing them shouting out the names of characters from various cartoons, it occurred to him that maybe he had a distorted view of how special this family was.

Together, Nishi and Miwako boiled the horsehair crabs. Miwako, who said her parents had grown up by the Sea of Okhotsk in Hokkaido, was clearly used to handling the creatures. As she deftly broke off their legs, explaining to Taro and Nishi what she was doing, her face was so full of life that she looked like a different person.

When Taro had heard that Miwako felt that the size of the house made her uneasy, he'd assumed, without any real reason, that she'd spoken out of spite, but when he saw her tucking enthusiastically into the crabs, he realized, to his surprise, that she really meant it. Just because you had the kind of life that everyone envied didn't mean that it was right for you. And yet Taro felt that if someone were to offer him the chance to live in this house, he would take them up on it without a second thought.

Taro wondered whether horsehair crabs, a local speciality in Hokkaido, were just a fact of life for Numazu now. And what about the graveyard in the woods buried in snow, where even the air was frozen? Would Numazu get accustomed to the idea of being buried there? He himself had felt more at home where he now lived than the place he'd grown up, and a picture flitted into Taro's head of Numazu and his wife in matching knitted hats, skiing together, smiling.

Everyone sat around the large low table on a green rug, eating the horsehair crabs, making hand-rolled sushi with salmon roe, tuna and salmon, with the three adults drinking beer. Miwako confessed that it had been a long time since she'd last had a drink, and asked Nishi several times if her face had reddened. The children, having finished off their meal with Hokkaido ice cream from Miwako's parents, seemed satisfied. They stood up and then began running and chasing each other around the living room, excited by the presence of the visitors.

Round and round and round they went, screeching and laughing. Miwako told them to stop, but her words had no effect on the kids, who seemed to be getting more and more absorbed by their game of tag. They kept on running, chasing after one another, as if caught up in a whirlpool. From time to time they would call out, "Wait!" or "You can't catch me!", sometimes switching roles, but however many times they went round, the game showed no signs of ending.

Eventually, the fact that the children weren't remotely getting tired of the game started to freak Taro out a little bit, and he began to feel like the great forty-square-metre room with its Indian-style wooden panels above the lintel was itself revolving. Noticing that Nishi was glaring at him, he suddenly remembered the plan to knock over the beer glass. But in that very moment, Taro saw Haruki come flying towards the table, and he let out a gasp.

Haruki landed hard on Nishi's back, and Nishi went crashing headfirst into the table. Not just Nishi's beer glass, but the other glasses and plates also went flying, and a chorus of breaking dishes rang out across the room. From where he lay draped across Nishi's shoulders, Haruki yelled out in surprise, then flung himself backwards. Yuna stood stock still behind where Nishi lay slumped over the table.

Miwako screamed. Looking up at her screaming, her mouth wide open, Taro no longer had any doubt that she truly was a good-hearted person, just as Nishi had said.

Nishi slowly peeled herself off the table and sat up. There was a shard of glass sticking out of her left arm. Her sleeve was rolled up, and the skin between her wrist and her elbow was cut in several places. There was blood on her face as well.

Seeing this, Miwako, who had come to Nishi's side, shrieked again, at which Haruki and Yuna both burst into tears.

"I'm okay, really," Nishi said, using her right arm that was free from glass to wipe the blood from the left side of her forehead. A trickle was running down to her ear, as if it had been painted there with a brush.

"Can I use your bathroom?"

"Hmm?" said Miwako, not understanding what she meant.

"Do you mind if I use your bathroom? I want to wash the blood off."

"Oh yes, of course," Miwako said, persuaded by the urgency in Nishi's tone, but as she was showing her the way, she stopped still in the doorway.

"Don't you think you should go to hospital?"

"Let her use the bathroom first," Taro cut in straight away. "She should wash the wounds off first in the bathroom."

For a couple of seconds Miwako stood frozen, then, coming back to herself, said, "Right, right. I'll bring her something to change into."

This, too, Taro challenged.

"I think it'd be better to clear this stuff up first. It's dangerous to leave it like this, with the kids around. I'll make sure she's okay."

Confronted by someone so dead set on achieving their objective, even after sustaining such injuries, Taro felt like he couldn't sit back and do nothing. How long was it since he'd had this feeling of wanting to help someone? Since he'd had this almost dutiful sense that he had to step in and do something for another person? Taro put his arm around Nishi, who had got slowly to her feet, and the two of them went out of the room. Down the hall and on the right, he opened the door to the washroom. Nishi had shown him the plan of the house, so he knew where all the rooms were.

They passed the washing machine and the sink, a double-bowled affair that was different from the one in the photo book, and opened the frosted glass door at the back of the room. When Taro flicked the light switch, the lime-green space instantly rose in front of them. For the first time ever, Nishi saw the bathroom. There were the tiles coating the entire space, the slow gradation from forest to lime green. The curved lines of colour covering the walls and the rim of the bathtub came together and overlapped with one another, so that even the air itself seemed stained a pale green.

Unlike the shot in *Spring Garden*, though, it was now evening, so there was no light from the window. Even during the day, Taro thought, most of the light would have been blocked by the concrete wall outside, which hadn't been there twenty years ago. Under the lights of the room, the greens of the tiles in front of them now were dull and flat. Taro felt a vague sense of disappointment. It was just a bathroom—just someone's bathroom. There was a plastic children's ball, an enamel washbowl with a cartoon character on it, and shampoo, conditioner and liquid soap that had been decanted into plain dispensers.

It was the bathroom of a house in which a young, wealthy family lived in 2014.

Seeming to have forgotten about the splinter of glass in her arm, Nishi had sat down on the rim of the bathtub and was looking around the small room. Her lips were parted slightly, and behind her glasses, her eyes had a dim gleam to them, a bit like she had fallen into a trance. The blood running down from the cut on her forehead had already dried a blackish red. Then Taro noticed a faint smile on her lips. He remembered what she'd said before: *I've always had luck on my side.*

Unfortunately, though, Nishi had forgotten about the compact camera she'd slipped into her pocket expressly to take photographs of the green-tiled bathroom. Instead, she tried simply to imprint the scene in her mind.

Afterwards Miwako called a taxi, and Taro accompanied Nishi to a hospital with a 24-hour accident and emergency clinic. She was made to wait for a while, but didn't complain about the pain. Instead, she seemed in a state of mild frenzy, and kept on talking about the bathroom tiles.

"What can I use to recreate those colours? That's the big question. I guess maybe watercolour acrylics would be best. Though I might need to use some kind of special effects on the image, maybe. What do you think?"

"I know nothing about art."

"I thought you might say that. I guess that rather than drawing in each individual tile, it might be better off capturing it generally, getting the overall balance of colour.

Actually, maybe overlapping layers of coloured pencil could work."

"It was just like in the photo, right?"

Nishi gave no reply.

They heard the siren of an ambulance, and then a patient was carried in on a stretcher. At the reception desk, an old man was complaining about something, repeating the same words over and over.

The cuts on Nishi's arms were deep, and she got a total of eleven stitches in three different places. Luckily, maybe thanks to the protection offered by her glasses, the damage done to her face was minor. The cut above her cheekbone didn't need stitches.

While Nishi and Taro were waiting to be charged for the treatment, Miwako's husband Yosuke appeared. It was the first time Taro had met him. He was a tall, polite man with a classically handsome face. He apologized very simply to Nishi, and paid all the hospital fees. Then he drove them back to their block of flats in his navy German sports car. Both Nishi and Taro were impressed by how nice it felt to ride in it. The following day, the whole Morio family appeared on Taro's doorstep, apologizing and thanking him. Haruki said in a loud clear voice, "I'm very sorry," though he didn't look up, so Taro knelt down and patted his head.

■　　■　　■

A week after, Nishi invited Taro to go over to the Morios' to see if there was any of their furniture or appliances that he wanted. They were giving it away. The cut on Nishi's face had mostly healed, and she said the stitches on her arm would be removed in three days' time. At the Morios', Miwako served them pancakes, smothered in maple syrup. It was Taro's policy not to touch home-made cookies and cakes, but he felt like he could hardly refuse when they were set down right in front of him, so he ate one on behalf of his pancake-loving colleague at work. Reciting to himself the words of praise his colleagues had lavished on Miwako's cooking, he managed to finish the whole thing.

Miwako explained that there was a lot of furniture in the house they were moving into in Fukuoka already, and it would be no mean feat transporting all this stuff, so she'd be positively grateful if they'd take it off her hands. When Taro checked that she meant for free, Miwako laughed and said, "I wish I could be as straightforward as you!"

Nishi took one of the two green armchairs in the sun-room, a steam oven and the bread-making machine.

Taro decided to take the other green armchair, the corner sofa occupying the centre of the living room, the ottoman, the reclining sofa on the first floor, and a chair like an enormous cushion, as well as the large refrigerator.

Over ten years ago, back when he was still living in Osaka, Taro had visited a cafe that featured remakes of the various chairs and sofas seminal in the history of furniture design, and ever since, had nursed the desire to be in a room of chairs and sofas of all kinds. It seemed like the opportunity had finally arrived.

A few days later, with the help of Yosuke Morio and one of his employees, Taro moved the various chairs and sofas to his flat in View Palace Saeki III. They took up so much space that there was barely an inch of his flat left that wasn't occupied by seating. From that day on, Taro spent almost all of his time at home sitting on one of the sofas or chairs. He placed a board on top of the ottoman and used it as a table. When it was time to sleep, he alternated between the reclining and the corner sofas. Curling up on the sofa sandwiched between the seat cushion and the backrest, he felt like an animal in a nest.

He wondered if this was how the potter's wasp larva inside the little vase had felt.

Taro asked Mrs Snake if she wanted to take a look around the Morios' house to see if there were any furniture that took her fancy, but she refused firmly, saying that she was at an age now where she had to be getting rid of things rather than getting more things. He'd got the impression from peering inside her room that she wasn't somebody who required a lot of furniture anyway, so her answer was expected. He gave her a ticket to an art exhibition that he'd received from one of his sweet-toothed colleagues, and she seemed very pleased. She said she'd not yet started looking for her next flat.

Nishi's movers came on Tuesday, while Taro was at work, and by the time he got home the Dragon Flat was empty. With the door shut, it didn't look immediately any different from how it had the previous day, but the darkness of the windows was not the darkness of a place in which someone lived. It was an empty sort of darkness, a darkness that seemed to say that there was nothing behind it at all.

Late that night, Taro got a short email from Nishi:

Thanks so much for your help with seeing the bathroom. I really owe you one for that. View Palace Saeki III is a great place to live, and I hope you enjoy the rest of your time there. I guess the gardens in Mrs Saeki's and the blue house will soon be full of the joys of spring! I envy you getting to see that.

The email also included a couple of links to websites featuring comic strips she'd drawn and revealing her pen name.

At the same time that Nishi and the Morios moved out, Mrs Saeki's son moved into the Saeki house. He came over to Taro's flat to introduce himself, and to tell Taro that he was very sorry but he was going to ask him to move out.

He had a round face that seemed like a mismatch with his height of almost six feet. He said that he had just retired, and needed to have various consultations with people about what to do with the land, as well as sorting through things in the house, so he had decided to move back for a while. His mother was doing well in a nearby care home, and he was planning to sell the land that the house and the flats sat on, the entirety of which would be converted into new flats. He handed Taro his business card: TORAHIKO SAEKI. The first part of his name, Tora, meant "tiger".

"This is going out on a bit of a limb," Taro said, "but do your brother or sister's names happen to use the characters for 'cow' or 'rabbit'?"

"I'm an only child," Torahiko said, in a clipped way. "I'm single and I have no relatives that I can rely on, so I need to clear things up properly with this house while I can. After I go, there'll be no one else around, so I've got to do what I can now. A bird fleeing the nest must leave no mess behind him, as they say."

This guy's a crafty one, Taro heard a voice in his head say. The voice was his own, but of course he didn't say the words out loud, nor did he yet really understand what they meant.

"Did you happen to know Mr Gyushima and Ms Umamura who used to live in the house behind you some time ago, maybe twenty years or so?"

"Oh yes, those oddballs. I knew of them. They released some kind of photo book and for a while afterwards there were young people turning up here to see the house. They only lived there for a year or two. My mother is something of a busybody, so she'd ask them over for a meal or a cup of tea from time to time. Once they came to borrow our birdcage, I think."

"With the bird inside?"

"We did used to have a budgie, but that would have been after it died. I imagine by that point my mother would just have been using the cage for flowers."

"Do you still have that cage?"

"Who knows? It might be put away somewhere, but I'm not sure."

Back inside his flat, after the man had gone, Taro leafed through the pages of *Spring Garden*. The birdcage was featured in three of the shots, but it was out of focus in all of them, and the outline of the bird, which could have been a parrot or parakeet or budgie, was blurred. Taro squinted at the photos, but could not bring the cage into focus.

Three days later, a gardening company arrived at Mrs Saeki's house and cut back the trees in the garden drastically. They also totally removed the ivy that was growing up the concrete wall.

■ ■ ■

It was February when I went to visit Taro. Three years had passed since we'd last seen each other, which was when we'd gone to our home town for the sixth anniversary of our father's death. At that time, I spent three days in the flat my mum lives in now, not the one on the twelfth floor of the municipal estate we'd grown up in, but a fourth-floor flat in a private block from which you could see that tower. That was the first time I heard about Taro's divorce.

In February, I was getting ready for a trip abroad. I work as a teacher in a college in Nagoya, and my annual holiday overseas is the thing I look forward to all year. The plan was that I would go over to my friend's house in Yokohama, where we would meet with another friend, and the three of us would then go to Narita for a flight to Taiwan, but because of heavy snow all transportation to Narita was stopped, and when we contacted the airlines they said they had no idea when our flight would take off, so we decided by majority vote to abandon the holiday. When I got in touch with my mother to tell her that, she said that since I was in Tokyo, I should go and check on Taro. There were major delays on the trains from Yokohama to Setagaya and it was a major pain to get there, as I began complaining to Taro, who had come to meet me at the station, the moment I saw him.

Taro responded in his usual half-hearted way, saying things like "really" and "oh" in a way that left you unsure if he was really listening to what you were saying. He seemed to have put on a bit of weight since the last time I'd seen him.

It was past three in the afternoon, but there was almost no one outside. The low-hanging sky was smothered with grey clouds, and everything around was snow as far as the eye could see. There was a strong wind, and even under an umbrella, my coat quickly turned white. The snow was already a good twenty centimetres deep, and our feet were buried in it. Taro, who I'd made carry my suitcase, was especially suffering. Midway home, I slipped and fell into the snow, which made Taro laugh. We saw several snowmen and what was, I guessed, supposed to be a snow grotto, though it looked more like a hole in the ground. I remembered once making a snow grotto at the ski slope that someone had taken us to. Thinking that Taro must share the memory, I grew excited and said what fun that had been, hadn't it, but Taro could only remember the skiing part. That was twenty-five years ago.

By the time we finally reached View Palace Saeki III, my coat and boots were soaked through with melted snow, and my fingers and toes were beginning to ache. For the first time, I saw Taro's Pig Flat. It was less messy than I'd expected, but I was shocked to see the entire room taken up with sofas and armchairs. The padded green armchair took up the middle of the hall, and the central tatami room contained the large corner sofa, which was turned to face the ottoman and the reclining sofa. The majestic silver fridge-freezer, which seemed to occupy half the kitchen, also took me by surprise. It was the kind that could freeze food to a specific temperature so it could then be cut without thawing it first. I'd heard about them, and had been wanting one myself, so I kept opening and closing the door of the freezer, saying how envious I was. Taro made vague noises: "ah", "yeah", "hmm", "I know". I knew that he secretly felt quite proud of himself for having a fridge like that.

After I'd finished my inspection of the fridge, I noticed that there was a book of photos on top of the ottoman. From its binding, it looked like a large children's book; it was called *Spring Garden*. Seeing my interest, Taro said, "That's the house just over there."

"Is it?"

"You could at least pretend to be surprised."

"If there's photos of a house, it stands to reason that the house exists somewhere in the world, surely."

"But look! It's just over there."

I walked to the door that led onto the balcony where Taro was pointing. Past the snow piled up on the concrete wall and the branches of the tree, and through the snow that was still falling at a slant, I could see the corner of the sky-blue house. It was already starting to get dark outside.

"Looks like it's pretty big."

"The person who gave me that book is the same age as you. She moved out recently, though."

On a board on top of the ottoman I arranged the ham, cheese and Baumkuchen that I'd got from my friend, and I opened a can of beer. Taro lounged around on the corner sofa, alternating between the middle and the end, and I went for the reclining sofa, sitting with my feet to the side or my knees up in front of me. If our mother was here, I thought, she would tell us off for sitting like slobs. It also struck me that I was far past the age when my mother would speak to me like that. And yet, the way that we were behaving wasn't so different from when we were kids, I thought to myself, and it was possible that someone watching us right now would find the sight ridiculous, or even kind of creepy. As he told me the story of the woman in the Dragon Flat, the house behind his flat, and the Morios who lived there, Taro would occasionally pick up *Spring Garden* and flick through it, then put it down again.

As it happened, I had seen *Spring Garden* before. A friend of mine in high school had been a big fan of Taro Gyushima's. She didn't really care about the adverts he made—she was more concerned with him as a man. Seeing the photos of him that accompanied his interviews, she'd come to think that he was her idea of the perfect guy. Naturally, she didn't like Kaiko Umamura at all. She hated the way she always acted cute and dumb, and said her name was weird. When I suggested that Kaiko Umamura was a stage name, probably the name of her character in the theatre troupe, my friend said she couldn't possibly get along with someone who would choose a name like that. In her mind, Kaiko Umamura could do nothing right.

"What do you reckon he's doing in this one?"

Taro opened the book at the page with the photo of Taro Gyushima digging a hole in the garden and showed it to me.

"Who knows. Maybe he was trying to make a pond."

"A pond..." said Taro, in a way that suggested that wasn't something that had ever occurred to him. He seemed so taken by the idea that he went on staring at the photo for a while.

It was night now, but the snow reflected the light from the flat, giving it a faint glow. It felt a bit as if we'd come to a hot-spring resort in one of the snowier parts of the country. True, Taro's flat was absolutely nothing like the traditional Japanese-style rooms you'd find in a hot spring, and it was over ten years since I'd been to a hot spring in the snow, but still, that was the thought that went drifting through my mind.

"It's about the right size to bury a dog in, don't you reckon?"

Still staring at the photo of the garden, Taro started telling me about Numazu and Cheetah. I instantly thought of Peter. Peter was a stray dog that we'd kept in the place where the motorbikes were parked in the municipal estate, back when I'd just started primary school. A bunch of boys from the estate a bit older than me, third and fourth years at my school, would bring it food and things. But then one day, after a few weeks, I came back from school and Peter was gone. I heard from the other kids that he'd been taken to the pound. Someone carved PETER into the trunk of a nearby camphor tree. I doubt that anyone else could have deciphered the strokes, but we all knew what it said, and what it meant. I would think of him every time I saw the cuts in that tree.

On the estate, the other kids and I always hung around in a big group. There was someone from the same year as me at school on each of the floors of the block, and we were always fighting for space in the titchy little parks in the estate grounds. The school we went to, which they were now considering closing down and merging with another school, was cramped with forty-five desks in a single classroom. There was barely space to move, and while there was expansion work going on, we had our lessons in prefab classrooms. Anywhere you went in that poky part of town, you would see someone you knew. I was always a part of a crowd. And yet, strangely enough, I never talked about Peter with any one of my classmates.

"I still feel sad when I think about him now," I said to Taro.

"I don't think he got taken to the pound, you know. He was white with brown patches and droopy ears, right?

When I went round to Matsumura's house in year four, he was there. Some of the kids from the estate had asked Matsumura's brother to take him home, and he did."

"Wow, I never knew that. When I told my friends at high school about it, I went on and on about how horrible they were for taking him away. And it wasn't even true!"

"I think he probably lived to a good old age. Matsumura used to live next to the house in Ni-chome. You know, the one that was set on fire by that land-shark. They moved right behind the school just before it happened. I remember his mum saying how lucky they'd been and stuff."

"Oh, that place! I went to see it a week before it was burned down, when a truck ran into it. We were playing in North Park and there was this huge noise, so we ran to have a look, just in time to see the driver jumping into another car and escaping. The guy in the house chased after him, but I bet he got away. That was a dirty trick to try and get him to move out."

"I have the feeling I heard about that from someone else, but I have absolutely no memory of it."

"You'd only have been two or so at that time. I bet the people living in the flats now have no idea that all that stuff went on back in the day."

"You know, I wonder if anything would turn up if you dug around the back garden."

"There've been a few different people living there since then, right?"

"Yep, three since this book."

"It's going to go up for rent again, isn't it? Why don't you rent it with someone else? It's cool these days, sharing houses."

"I can't live with other people."

"Oh yeah, I'd forgotten you're uptight about that kind of stuff. Remember how you used to cry and say you couldn't sleep unless it was pitch black, so I had to turn out the nightlight."

"I didn't cry about it."

Taro hadn't joined me in drinking beer. He was drinking green tea from a plastic bottle.

Looking out of the window as if he was checking something, he said, "You once told me I'd be able to sleep if I watched the red lights of the factory."

"I don't remember that at all. It was probably something I made up to shut you up."

At first I'd had the top bunk, but when Taro started school, he said he wanted it, and my parents made us switch because I was older. Until then, I'd always looked out at the city lit up with those red lights before I went to sleep. Those pulsating lights, they always seemed to me like the night was breathing.

"It's amazing that we managed to live all that time in the same room."

"We didn't know what it was like to have our own space yet, that's why."

It was at that moment that I realized that I would never again live with Taro. I felt pretty sure that he was realizing the same thing at the same time.

"Anyway, with those kinds of houses there's usually a rule that you're not allowed to share with people who aren't family. You don't pass the landlord's inspection."

Nodding along with what Taro was saying, I opened my last can of beer. Then I picked up the photo book.

"Don't you know anyone who'd want to live in a place like this? If it was someone you knew who moved in, you could go round when you wanted."

"I can't think of anyone."

"Yeah, I thought you might say that."

"What the hell do you mean by that?"

"It looks really big."

"This whole flat would fit inside the hall."

"There aren't any photos of them eating."

Taro, who was sitting on top of the backrest of the corner sofa, looked at me with an expression like a startled cat. It was a look that somehow made me think of our childhood. I opened the book and held it up in front of his face.

"These two live together in this house, but there isn't a single photo of them eating. Or of any kind of food, either."

Taro flipped through the pages and mumbled, "It's true."

Then he said, "I wonder if Nishi noticed that."

"She must have," I said, but Taro kept on looking at the book.

I'd run out of both beer and food. The snow-covered streets outside were totally still. Quite possibly, I thought, this part of the city was quiet even when it wasn't snowing. From time to time, we heard a mound of snow falling from a roof or a branch somewhere. The sound was like heaviness itself. The great mass of white crystals sucked away all warmth from the air. The temperature of the houses, the trees, the utility poles, the asphalt, the air, the night, all went on falling.

The next day, it was glorious weather that made the previous day seem like it had been a dream, and melted snow fell from the edges of the buildings like rain. Taro and I took a pot and a frying pan outside, and made a very minimal attempt at clearing away the snow. It was the first time, in fact, I'd ever cleared snow. There were no signs of life from either the sky-blue house or the concrete one, but people from the house diagonally opposite came out and started clearing the snow too, and I felt somehow relieved to see that there were people actually living in the area, given how deserted it had been the day before. I wanted to meet Mrs Snake, but it seemed like she was out.

In the evening, after Taro had voted for the next governor of Tokyo, we went to a yakitori restaurant near the station. It turned out, though, that a lot of food supplies hadn't been delivered because of the bad weather, and almost everything I wanted to order was unavailable. Taro surprised me by eating the leeks in the *negima* skewers, rather than picking them out from between the pieces of chicken as he'd used to do.

When we got back to the Pig Flat, I suggested that since the place was so cramped, I should take the green armchair off him. I knew that Taro wouldn't bother to put up a struggle about this, and, as I thought, he replied, "Yeah, fine, if you want." As I made the arrangements with the delivery service to have it transported to Nagoya, I had the thought that the next time I saw Taro, not only would he not be living here, but this room, along with the rest of the flat, would no longer exist.

The day after I went back home, Taro began searching for a new flat on estate sites. He knew he had to hurry and find somewhere to live, but he had no idea of the sort of place he wanted to move to, or where. Clicking on the SIMILAR RESULTS images and adverts that popped up in his search results, he found himself looking at a whole house in a town called Teppomachi in Yamagata Prefecture, way out in the countryside in the north of Japan. The picture showed a smallish, two-storey house, surrounded by banks of snow.

Taro realized that, if he wanted to, he could live somewhere like this. That was to say, he could choose a place he'd never been, that he knew nothing about whatsoever. He didn't know if he'd be able to keep living there or not, but for what it was worth, he could at least move in. Move into a house like this listing with a bedroom that looked perfect for lying around in. He clicked on the various images of the house, one by one, and saw last of all a photo of the bathroom. Seeing the walls with their chequered black and white tiles, Taro decided that he'd put off searching for a flat.

A month later, I was back in Nagoya. I finished work for the day and came back to my fifth-floor flat. Sitting in my green armchair, one half of a matching pair that had once belonged to the Morios and was now shared by Nishi and me, I drank a can of beer. I wasn't concerned about my alcohol intake like Taro was, but I had noticed recently that my handwriting was beginning to resemble my father's. The older I got, the more my writing looked like a row of little drunk people walking. When I caught sight of a note I'd scribbled a while back, I would sometimes be sure that my father had written it. My father hadn't taught me to write, so why my writing should gradually grow to look like his was puzzling. When I'd visited Taro's flat and caught sight of his handwriting, I'd seen that it didn't look like either of our parents'.

I opened up my laptop, and after doing the usual survey of my Twitter feed and the blogs I always looked at, checking up on how my friends who lived nearby and a cat that belonged to someone in Toronto I'd never met were doing that day, I put on a DVD that I'd rented. It was a drama based on events of the Second World War. After I'd been watching it for thirty minutes, it dawned on me that I'd seen it before, some time ago.

Stuffing my hand down between the arm and the seat of the chair, I brushed against something hard. I dug it out, and a small white object like a pebble fell onto the floor. It was a tooth—a baby tooth, with no roots. It looked like a front tooth, but whether it was top or bottom, and what number it was, I had no idea.

I remembered something people used to say when I was a kid: throw your bottom teeth into the sky, and bury your top ones in the ground. It definitely could have been a top tooth, and even if it was a bottom one, I figured that if I threw it into the sky it would come tumbling down anyway, so I decided to bury it, and stepped outside to find a good place. The daytime had been freezing cold and the wind strong enough to knock over the bicycles parked in the street, but the evening air was very mild.

When I'd looked at the weather forecast earlier that evening, it had showed that the temperature in Tokyo was almost ten degrees different from that in Osaka. The line dividing the cold of a few hours ago from this warm air must have moved over the place where I was now, midway between those two cities.

I left my apartment and walked down the hill. For a long time, I'd fantasized about living in a place with a hill. I liked the sound of it, and that was in fact why I'd chosen my current flat. The hill even had a flight of steps in the middle. When the person from the estate agency had first brought me here, I'd thought that flight of steps strangely touching. It had seemed to me like something right out of a comic book.

Going down the hill, I remembered Nishi's latest comic strip, which Taro had turned me on to. The frames had popped up one by one on the screen of my laptop. The strip recounted a Chinese folk tale about a heavy-drinking fisherman who shared his saké with the river and had his kindness repaid by the ghost of someone who had drowned there, updated and set in modern-day Tokyo. Nishi's illustrations were cute. Her people were often a bit snake-like.

Walking beside a bus lane, I passed someone going the other way with their dog. It was a kind of dog I'd never seen before. Its face looked like that of a collie, but its body was small, and it had short legs.

Its owner was talking to it the whole way. "Are you tired? Can you keep going? Do you want to go home? No, you want to keep walking, do you?"

Six hours after I went out to find a place to bury the tooth, Taro climbed over the railing of his balcony and entered the courtyard with the NO ENTRY sign. It seemed as though the wind had finally died down. He'd turned off the lights in his flat before coming out, so he had to squint in order to see in the darkness. He piled up the concrete blocks that were placed in the corner of the courtyard and used them to get a leg up onto the wall. On his back, he carried a cloth bag with the things he needed, a strap over each of his shoulders. With a foot against the wall, he turned around and saw that there was one flat with its lights on— the second from the left on the first floor. Taro had seen Mrs Snake at lunchtime that day, for the first time in two weeks. She had been to the exhibition Taro had given her the ticket for, and had been given a special prize for being the 10,000th visitor. She seemed really pleased about this, which also made Taro pleased. Would she be awake at a time like this? Maybe she was the opposite of Taro, and couldn't sleep unless the lights were on.

Taro climbed over the wall, and came down on the side of the sky-blue house. The palms of his hands stung slightly where he'd scraped them on the dried vines that were now all that remained of the ivy. He walked slowly along the gap between the wall and the house. The gravel crunched beneath his feet.

When he came out into the garden, the sky yawned wide above him. Several stars were twinkling. Lit up from below by the lights of the city, the clouds that had come blowing in from the west were a hazy white.

Clouds at night didn't invite Taro's vision of climbing on top of the clouds, either. Rather, they made him think of a photograph that an astronaut living on a space station had posted on Twitter. The surface of the earth at night, seen from the darkness of space, was like a map rendered in particles of light. This city where Taro was now would have been a great big cluster of those particles. Taro found it impossible to believe that the lights of this place where he now was could be seen from so far away. He remembered being stunned when he'd read in a book as a kid that if you made a model of the globe with a diameter of two metres, and accurately represented the contours of its surface, even Everest would only be as high as a thick coating of paint. The idea, then, that you could see the lights of this city from space, this city that was really no more than a blip on the earth's surface, seemed unthinkable.

A view he'd once seen from a plane window floated into his mind: floating in a sea of darkness, little clusters of lights. The lights marked the towns where people lived.

The moon had already sunk from view, but there was a streetlight just beyond the wall of the house, so the garden was bright enough for his digging. It felt big. The twisted branches of the crepe myrtle, which had not yet come into leaf, cast shadows on the ground. Taro crouched in front of the plum tree. He had slipped the garden trowel he'd bought in the DIY shop into the back pocket of his jeans. He stuck the trowel into the ground that was littered with plum petals, and began digging the soil. It was faintly warm. When he had been digging for about ten minutes, the end of his trowel hit something hard. Taro brushed away the earth with his hand, and dug around the thing carefully.

It was a stone. A round stone, about the size of an egg. There were lots of them. He kept unearthing stone after stone of almost the same shape. By the time there were none left for him to dig, there was a heap of them on the edge of his hole.

Where the stones had been, Taro laid the mortar and pestle and the potter wasp's nest he'd brought from his flat. With his bare hands he scooped up the soft soil he'd dug up and let it fall onto the objects in the hole. Once the mortar and pestle and the wasp nest were no longer visible, he returned the rest of the soil with the trowel.

Taro wished he'd asked his father if he'd ever been to Tokyo, but he couldn't think of a time when there would have been a chance to ask him that kind of thing. He definitely remembered his dad saying that he liked plum trees, though. He'd said that he much preferred plum blossoms to the cherry blossoms that everyone in Japan made such a big fuss about. Taro had agreed with him, and his father had said that was "unlike him". At the time, Taro had thought that his father meant that it was unlike Taro to agree with him, but maybe that hadn't been what he'd been trying to say. Perhaps he was saying that it was unlike

Taro to own up to liking flowers, or unlike him to give an opinion at all. From now on, Taro thought, he wouldn't have the sight of the mortar and pestle to remind him of his father. He'd have to remember him at other times. That probably made sense. After all, his father had never even laid eyes on that mortar and pestle.

When Taro brought his face up close to the slightly smaller tree alongside the plum, he saw that buds were beginning to form on its branches. It was the Hall crabapple Nishi had spoken of. At first he'd found its name a bit cumbersome, but now he could remember it, along with an image of its deep pink-coloured blossoms as they appeared in the illustrated guide to plants Mrs Snake had given him.

Nishi wouldn't be able to see it in bloom this year, but he would. He could take a photo of it and send it to her.

The window facing the balcony on the first floor was reflecting the dawn sky.

Taro climbed back up the concrete wall and, holding onto the gutter for support, found his way onto the second-floor balcony. The old ground-floor windows leading to the sunroom had been replaced with new ones, but not those on the first floor. When Taro had gone into the bedroom with the balcony to collect the reclining sofa, Mr Morio had told him that the lock on the door was broken, and you could open the door with a good thump. Now Taro did just that, hitting the place near the lock several times. He rattled the door and saw that the lock, shaped like an ear, had come undone. He opened the glass door, took off his shoes and put them in the cloth bag on his back, then stepped onto the tatami.

If Nishi's favourite room in the house was the bathroom, then Taro's was this bedroom. Because of his habit of sprawling out on the floor in whatever room he happened to be in, he liked rooms with tatami floors, which were softer and nicer for lying on. There were five photos of this room in the book, including one of Kaiko Umamura doing a bridge right in the middle of the room. Her head was touching the floor, and her arms were folded across her chest. She was smiling. In another shot, she was mid-cartwheel, moving so fast that the photo was blurred, and yet, even amid the blur, you could see the gleam in her eyes.

The room was spacious. It still smelt a little of the rushes that were used to make the tatami. Taro sat down on the tatami, pulled out a fleece blanket from his bag, and rolled himself up in it. Facing towards the window, he could see the sky. It occurred to him that he had never once seen a shooting star. He could hear crows cawing.

He was woken by the sun, now high up in the sky. When he checked his phone, he saw it was past ten.

He could hear noises from downstairs, and several different voices. Still lying on the floor, he listened carefully, but couldn't make out what was being said. Figuring that potential residents had probably come for a viewing, he felt anxious, and got up. He went down a few steps on the staircase, trying to gauge the situation, and peeped down through the handrail from a spot where he would not be visible from the floor below.

There was a man in a blue uniform with yellow letters on his back that read METROPOLITAN POLICE DEPARTMENT. He wore his baseball cap of the same blue backwards.

"We've found a woman's body in the garden," a man's voice was saying. The voice had a strange clarity to it, and Taro felt as though he'd heard it somewhere before.

"Did you hear any noises at all last night?"

"No, nothing at all," said a young woman's voice.

Trying not to make any noise, Taro went down another step, and then another. When he reached the midway landing, he saw a man in a suit standing next to the criminal investigator and, opposite them, a woman.

The woman had her eyes cast down. She kept putting a hand up to touch her long hair. From the side, she looked a lot like Kaiko Umamura in the photo of her reading in a wicker chair in the sunroom.

"What time did you get home yesterday?"

"What are you trying to say, sir?"

"Okay, and cut!" said a voice, and the floor suddenly filled with commotion. The lights dropped, and three men dressed in blue uniforms moved up and down the corridor. Someone, either the director or another member of the crew, was giving directions for the next scene to be shot.

Only the woman stayed in the same place, her head now raised. From the front, she didn't look like Kaiko Umamura after all. In fact, she looked more like Nishi. But that thought only stayed in Taro's mind for a second, and then he remembered the actress's name.

She looked Taro straight in the eye, and made a gesture with her hand, as though lifting something up. Taro eventually realized she was telling him to go back upstairs. He nodded at her. He saw her mouth move, but failed to catch what she said.

Taro went up the stairs and back into the bedroom, shouldered his bag, then stepped out onto the balcony. Looking down from there, he saw two vans filling the parking spaces, and members of the crew carrying lights and microphones up and down the street. When would it be screened? he wondered. He knew it usually took a long time after filming before programmes actually made it onto the TV.

He climbed over the balcony railing, and holding on to the gutter for support, managed to get a footing on the concrete wall. With his hands on the side of the sky-blue house, he walked carefully along the top of the wall. It was a clear, sunny day and the temperature was rising. He felt sweat on his back.

When he reached the border with the Saeki house, the concrete vault, and View Palace Saeki III, Taro stopped. With his hands still touching the blue wooden boards of the house, he looked over towards his block of flats. On her first-floor balcony, Mrs Snake was hanging out her washing. There was one piece of fabric in navy and one in dark green, although what shape those clothes would take when Mrs Snake put them on, he had no idea. Other than the Snake Flat, and the Pig Flat in the right corner of the ground floor, all the flats were now empty.

Their windows and the balconies were arranged in two neat lines. The sunlight shone into the windows, all shaped exactly the same. He could see the lines dividing light from shade falling on the walls of the first-floor flats, and on the tatami of those on the ground-floor flats. Nothing changed. Nothing made a sound. Only the boundary lines between the light and the shade shifted, like a sundial.

Taro's flat was full of sofas and chairs. The whole place was buried in ivory-coloured fabric. Sitting on top of the wall and looking into his room, he could see the enormous refrigerator gleaming silver. He remembered that there was tofu in there he had to eat today, before it went bad.

JAPANESE FICTION
AVAILABLE AND COMING SOON
FROM PUSHKIN PRESS

MS ICE SANDWICH
Mieko Kawakami

MURDER IN THE AGE OF ENLIGHTENMENT
Ryūnosuke Akutagawa

THE HONJIN MURDERS
Seishi Yokomizo

RECORD OF A NIGHT TOO BRIEF
Hiromi Kawakami

SPRING GARDEN
Tomoka Shibasaki

COIN LOCKER BABIES
Ryu Murakami

THE DECAGON HOUSE MURDERS
Yukito Ayatsuji

SLOW BOAT
Hideo Furukawa

THE HUNTING GUN
Yasushi Inoue

SALAD ANNIVERSARY
Machi Tawara

THE CAKE TREE IN THE RUINS
Akiyuki Nosaka